Buzza[illegible]ost

When Joe Trueman rides into Dry Bluff with the injured body of Doc Drummond thrown across his horse's back, he little realizes the trouble he is getting into. Drummond is just one more victim of Kettle and his gang of gunslicks, who threaten not only the town but the wagon-train route to Denver and beyond.

Dealing with Kettle is only the start. Behind Kettle looms the more menacing figure of Cush Vogler, and it's a long ride to Vogler's ranch, the Buckle M.

Menaced every step of the way, Trueman arrives in the nearby settlement of Buzzard Roost. Then things really get hot. As violence erupts and a range war breaks out between the Buckle M and the much smaller Two Bar Cross, the citizens must decide: do they have the nerve to dare stand by Trueman when the bullets fly?

By the same author

Pack Rat
Coyote Falls
Shotgun Messenger
Guns of Wrath
Six-Gun Nemesis
North to Montana
Back from Boot Hill
Tough Justice

Buzzard Roost

Colin Bainbridge

ROBERT HALE · LONDON

First published in Great Britain 2015

ISBN 978-0-7198-1493-8

Robert Hale Limited
Clerkenwell House
Clerkenwell Green
London EC1R 0HT

www.halebooks.com

Typeset by
Derek Doyle & Associates, Shaw Heath
Printed and bound in Great Britain by
CPI Antony Rowe, Chippenham and Eastbourne

CHAPTER ONE

The late afternoon was gloomy. Clouds scudded across a troubled sky. Down the trail a lone rider drew his horse to a halt and peered at a rickety signpost. *Dry Bluff: Wagons and Supplies.* He raised himself in the saddle and peered in the direction in which the sign was pointing, but he could see nothing. Settling back, he rode on. Across the back of his Steel Dust a man's body was slung. The rider, a man named Joe Trueman, had found him a little way off the trail. He had been shot, but he had been lucky. The bullet had scored his back, creating a nasty gash. The man was still unconscious, and when Trueman turned him over he saw that his face was swollen where he must have hit it on landing from his horse. There was no sign of the animal. Trueman bound his wound as best he could but he needed a doctor. Dry Bluff was out of his way, but it was the only place he would be likely to find one.

He rode on at a slow and steady pace, not wanting to do anything that might make the man's injury any worse. The sign had not said how far it was to the town. A considerable time seemed to pass and Trueman was beginning to wonder whether he might not have gone wrong, when he saw a faint glow ahead of him. Presently the shadowy forms of buildings began to show against the darkening skyline and he was soon riding past some outlying shacks and adobes. He carried on down the empty street, his horse's hoofbeats muffled by layers of dust. His eyes were fixed ahead but occasionally he glanced to right and left. The false-fronts ran on in an unbroken line, uneven and ragged, a continuation of the hard desert trail he had been riding. The whole place was deserted and he looked in vain for any sign of life or movement. Few lights showed, but above the creak of his saddle leather and the moaning of the wind he thought he detected other faint sounds. He came to a corner and, unexpectedly, the street opened on to a small square. Light spilled from a building in the corner and the sounds he had heard resolved themselves into the murmur of voices and the desultory tinkling of a piano. Over the entrance the words *Dragon Saloon* were scrawled in high faded letters. He rode up, dismounted, and tied his horse to the hitching rail. He checked that the wounded man was still unconscious, then stood for a moment, taking a last look about him before stepping up on to the low sidewalk and brushing through the batwing doors.

The atmosphere was thick with smoke, stale beer and sawdust. As he strode towards the bar the piano fell silent and the hum of voices was replaced by a palpable silence. Trueman quickly noted the layout of the place and the relative positions of the men at the tables. Three others were standing at the bar. In total there weren't as many of them as he would have expected – little more than a dozen – and his first impression was that they were not the typical type of clientele. They were a mean-looking bunch and they all packed iron. He was immediately on the alert: he knew he had walked into something. Keeping his eyes fixed ahead, he made his way to the bar. The three men fanned out as the barman appeared.

'Whiskey,' Trueman said.

The barman poured a drink and placed it in front of him. Trueman threw it back and ordered another. As the barman poured, he was conscious that the three men had placed themselves behind him and through the bar mirror he could see that a couple of men had taken up a position near the batwings.

'I need a doctor,' he said to the barman. 'Any idea where I might find one?'

'Kinda late, ain't it?' a voice said behind him. Trueman took a moment to sip some of the whiskey before slowly turning round.

'Yeah, but I still need a doctor.' The man facing him was thin as a paring.

'Ain't no doctor in this town,' he said. His two companions glanced at each other.

'Hell,' one of them quipped. 'What's your problem?'

'Looks to me like he's got screw-worm,' another one offered. Trueman waited a moment for the laughter to subside.

'Nope,' he replied, 'not screw-worm. Cholera. I got a wagon down the trail and it sure don't look good.' The reaction was instantaneous. The men dropped back and the barman moved away.

'You'd better get the hell outa here,' the thin man said. Trueman slung back the last of the whiskey.

'You're sure about that doctor?' he said.

'Just turn right round and beat it. And make sure that wagon don't come anywhere near Dry Bluff.'

Trueman turned away and began to move down the saloon. The men at the table shrank away and the two barring the exit had gone. He stepped through the batwings and out into the cool night air. For the time being he wasn't taking any more chances. Swinging into leather, he rode away, thinking as he did so that he hadn't paid for the drinks. The hostile reception he had received rankled with him and he didn't intend to let it drop. The more he thought about it, the angrier he became. He felt sure that he had been lucky to get away with his life. Only his quick thinking had saved him.

He rode further along the main street without seeing anybody. There was something wrong about the town. The streets were unnaturally deserted and the only saloon was full of gunslingers. Could there be a connection with the injured man he had found? Maybe it was none of his business, but somehow he felt as though he already had a stake in what was going on, whatever it was.

In the meantime, in spite of what he had been told, he still needed to find a doctor. There had to be one somewhere. He had almost reached the far end of town when he saw a light glimmering through the shutters of a building. There was a sign above the door: *Dry Bluff Epitaph.* For a moment he thought it was the undertaker and then he realized it was a newspaper office. Someone seemed to be still at work. Maybe he could offer some assistance. He stopped and considered whether to ask him for help, but then decided against it. In view of what had happened at the saloon, it might be a better idea to carry on riding and find some place to make camp outside of town. But he would be back.

Trueman had left everyone in the saloon in a state of considerable consternation. The desperadoes who made it their own had been thrown off balance and it took a few more drinks for them to regain something of their equilibrium.

'I've seen cholera before,' one of them commented. 'It ain't a pretty thing.'

'There were rumours about that last wagon train we robbed,' another one said, addressing the thin man who had spoken to Trueman. 'Maybe we'd better post a guard at either end of town. What do you think, Swain?'

Swain's expression was grim. 'Shut up, Dungan!' he snapped.

'I was only sayin'—'

Swain turned to face him. 'I said shut up! I need to think.'

'Looks like we might have made a mistake shootin' the doc,' another voice quipped. There was a ripple of laughter, but the man's words struck a false note.

'Maybe we'd better let Kettle know.'

'I should have shot that varmint!' Swain snapped. 'He was probably lyin'.'

'But what if he ain't?'

Swain threw back his glass of whiskey. He didn't like to admit it because it might weaken his position of dominance over the others, but he was out of his depth. He liked the issues to be simple. Gunning a man down in cold blood made sense to him, but in this case there were complications. His brain, already befuddled with drink, couldn't work things out. It made him frustrated but at the same time he was grateful for the chance to get out of having to make a decision.

'Maybe you're right,' he snapped. 'I'll go and have a word with Kettle myself.'

Without waiting for a response he turned and made his way up the stairs to the landing above. A little way down a short corridor was Kettle's room. Swain had seen the boss go up there earlier and he knew he had a woman with him. He needed to tackle the matter carefully. He swore silently to himself. Maybe he should have sent one of the others up. Hell, what was he supposed to say? He stood for a moment on the landing, but even as he braced himself he heard sounds coming from Kettle's room. They were unmistakable and as they increased in volume he thought better of his resolve and began to make his way back down the stairs.

'Did you tell him?' somebody said.

'Now ain't a good time,' he replied.

The man looked blankly at him, then an ugly grin spread across his features. Swain turned to the piano player.

'Why are you just sittin' there?' he rapped. The man looked flustered. 'Hell, what's this place come to. Give us a tune. Come on boys, drink up.'

The piano man began to strum the ivories. Somebody began to sing. In a little time, the incident involving Trueman was more or less forgotten, but Swain, still unsure of his ground, continued to nurse an obscure grievance.

*

Trueman rode till he was well clear of town and then set up camp by a stream in the shade of some cottonwood trees. As gently as he could he lifted the wounded man down from the horse and laid him on the ground, covered him with a blanket and, trying to make him as comfortable as possible, placed his saddle behind the man's head. Then he built a fire and laid some slabs of bacon in the pan. He filled his old iron pot with water and positioned it over the flames. He had just laid his food on a platter and was pouring coffee into his tin cup when he heard a grunt. He looked round to see in the firelight that the stranger had made an effort to sit up. The man's eyes were on him.

'Take it easy,' Trueman said.

'What happened?' the man asked in a low voice.

'You've been shot. I found you.'

The man grunted again.

'Hell, it hurts,' he said. He paused for a moment and then nodded in the direction of the fire. 'I could sure use some of that.'

'Grub?'

'Nope, just coffee.'

Trueman rose and walked over to his horse. He returned carrying a flask and another cup. He poured coffee into the cup, then laced it with whiskey from the flask.

'Here,' he said. The stranger took the cup. After he had swallowed a few mouthfuls he sank back against the saddle.

'How are you feelin'? Trueman said.

'Not too good, but it could've been worse.'

'Yeah. I took you into town to seek out a doctor, but I couldn't find one.'

'That ain't surprisin',' the man said. 'I'm the doc.'

Trueman nodded. 'Then I guess you know what needs to be done?'

'Did you do anythin'?'

'I cleaned it all up. The bullet cut quite deep, but it didn't enter. As far as I could see, there was nothin' broken.'

'Thanks,' the man replied. 'Then it's mainly a matter of keepin' it clean.'

'If you tell me what to do, I'll try dressin' it,' Trueman said.

'That's real good of you.' The doctor laid his cup on the ground. 'I'm Doc Drummond,' he announced.

'Joe Trueman. Pleased to make your acquaintance.'

Trueman cleared his plate and poured another cup of coffee for himself and Drummond. He was about to add some whiskey when he shrugged and handed the doctor the flask instead. For a while neither spoke. The wind was loud in the branches of the trees and the water rippled and splashed against the riverbanks. Eventually Trueman turned to the doctor.

'Have you got any idea who did it?' he asked. The doctor thought for a moment.

'Not exactly,' he replied. 'But I got a pretty good notion.'

'Yeah? Who?'

'A man named Kettle. He and his gang have taken over the town of Dry Bluff. I had it comin'.'

Trueman nodded. 'That kinda figures,' he said.

'What? You've come across Kettle before?'

'I stopped by the Dragon saloon. Let's just say it wasn't exactly a friendly welcome.'

'You were takin' a big risk,' Drummond replied. 'That's one of Kettle's favourite roosts.'

'Why did you say you figured you had it comin'?'

'It's what happens to anyone who stands in Kettle's way. I happened to have helped a few of his victims. I'm just surprised they didn't finish the job.'

'You were probably just a random target,'

'Kettle is bad and he has a lot of influence, but he ain't the main man. There's somebody else behind him. Have you ever heard the name Vogler?'

Trueman thought for a moment. 'Can't say that I have. But then, I ain't from round these parts.'

'Nobody knows anything much about him, but there's rumours. The wagon train route passes near Dry Creek. It's one reason for the town's existence. The days are soon comin' when the railroad will take over. I don't know what will happen to the town then, but that's another story. Just recently there have been a lot of attacks on wagon trains along the trail. A lot of it is small-time stuff – oxen and horses bein' stolen. I figure Kettle and other small-time gangs are the culprits, but they're doin' it at someone else's instigation, somebody who's reapin' most of the rewards. Vogler is the name that seems to crop up.' Drummond sank back again, drained by the effort of speaking.

Trueman considered his words. Vogler? He didn't think he had heard the name. He was brought round by the voice of Drummond speaking again.

'I appreciate you goin' out of your way to try and help me,' the doc said. 'Where were you headin'?'

'No place special. Just travellin'. Just passin' through.' Trueman paused for a moment. 'Leastways, that's what I *was* doin'. I got a notion now to stick around for a spell.'

'You'd do better to carry right on goin'.'

'How about you? If Kettle's planned on havin' you removed, he ain't gonna take kindly to seein' you back on the streets.'

Drummond suddenly made to sit up, but quickly lapsed back wincing with pain.

'I've spent a lot of years around Dry Bluff,' he said. 'I might leave of my own accord, but I don't intend Kettle or anyone else runnin' me out.'

'Funny sort of place to settle down,' Trueman said.

'Suits me,' Drummond replied. 'Or at least, it used to. I ain't so sure any more.'

Trueman smiled. The doctor's face was wrinkled and his hair was streaked with grey.

'Well,' he said, 'I guess we both feel the same way. I don't take to anyone tryin' to lean on me. Maybe you'd better tell me more about this Kettle *hombre*.'

The doctor grimaced.

'I sure will,' he said, 'but we'd better see to this wound first.' He paused and then glanced at Trueman with a spark in his eyes. 'I got medicines back at my place. It's a quiet spot a few miles out of town. If you intend stayin' around a while, you could put up with me and Rose. We got the room.'

He and Trueman exchanged glances.

'Rose?' Trueman queried.

'She's part Pawnee. She ain't my wife, but we have an understandin'.'

'How's she gonna feel if I show up?'

'She'll be grateful. Hell, seems like you saved my life.'

'I reckon she must be wonderin' what's become of you.'

'Yeah, I guess so. She's used to me keepin' odd hours with bein' a doctor and all. She'll be pleased to have company. Besides, stayin' over at my place would be lot more sensible than puttin' your own life on the line by showin' up in Dry Bluff.'

Trueman pondered his suggestion. 'Well,' he concluded, 'If you're sure I wouldn't be puttin' either of you out, maybe I could use your floor for a day or two, till I get things sorted.'

'You'd be plumb welcome. I tell you what. If you reckon that horse of yours is up to it, we could head there now. Rose can do the honours with the dressin' and I can fill you in with what I know about Kettle. It ain't much.'

'And Vogler,' Trueman responded. He glanced in the direction of the Steel Dust. 'I think the old fella can manage a few more miles. Just try and relax for a few minutes while I put out the fire and wash these things. Then we'll get movin'.'

Things had settled down at the Dragon saloon. Kettle's gunslicks had made themselves comfortable downstairs, while in the room above their boss reclined, his lusts finally sated, with his head on the pillow looking up at the shadowed ceiling. He turned aside to glance at the woman sleeping by his side and felt only distaste. It was the way he usually felt with any woman once she had served her purposes. But the feeling had deeper roots. By the standards of a two-bit gunslinger like Swain he was doing pretty well, but he had higher ambitions.

He swung his legs wide of the bed, pulled on his

trousers and walked across to a partly open door which gave on to a balcony. He leaned on the rail and looked down on the deserted streets. The wind had dropped and stars were showing. Beyond the town the prairie lay dark and empty. Away off across that sea of grass somewhere was Vogler's headquarters, the Buckle M. Vogler was involved in the cattle business, both raising and rustling the critters. But that was the tip of the iceberg. If there was anything shady going on in the whole region, you could be certain that Vogler was involved. Kettle was getting tired of working for him: stealing from wagon trains, robbing stagecoaches, all for Vogler's benefit. He was left to live off the gleanings.

In a sudden burst of anger he kicked at the balcony rail and leaned over to spit down on to the street below. One day he was going to be the boss. He began to think of how it would be when that time came to pass, until eventually, feeling better, he made his way inside. Slipping back into bed, he reached his hand to feel for the woman's heavy breasts. Yes, he was definitely feeling a whole lot better.

Trueman was relieved when Drummond's homely dwelling came into view. It wasn't easy riding double and he had to go carefully for fear of opening up the doctor's wound. It was a small two-storey building with a veranda running round three of its sides. It was set, however, in a sizeable tract of land, with an orchard at the back leading down to a brook. There was a light at one of the downstairs windows. Trueman drew up his horse and turned to his passenger.

'Looks like Rose is about,' he said, 'but we don't want to go scarin' the lady.'

'There ain't nothin' scares Rose,' Drummond replied. 'She ain't the type.'

'All the same. . . .'

Before Trueman could finish, and as if to answer his hesitation, the door of the house swung open and a female figure appeared on the veranda, carrying a shotgun.

'Who is it?' a thin voice called. 'I know you're there. Better say right out who you are before I drill you full of buckshot.'

'It's me,' Drummond called out. 'I got a friend along. He's called Trueman.'

The figure took a step forward and peered though the darkness.

'I think I see you, Jez. Why, where's your horse?'

Trueman urged the Steel Dust forward and stopped outside a fence which enclosed the yard.

'Drummond's injured,' he said. 'Help me get him down.'

The woman laid her gun against the wall of the house, stepped down from the veranda and came forward. As she approached Trueman got a clear view of her. She was small and thin with long hair turning from black to grey hanging down to her shoulders in a braid. She was wearing a faded nightdress but her feet were bare. Between them they got the doctor down from the horse and into the house.

'Put him on the sofa,' Rose said. Drummond was making the best of it, but Trueman could tell from the tightness of his expression how much pain he was feeling.

'Get my spare medicine bag,' Drummond murmured through clenched teeth. 'And boil up some water.'

While Rose was gone Trueman observed the house. It was tastefully decorated and he thought he could see Rose's touch in the choice of cushions, antimacassars and soft curtains, and in the arrangements of flowers which stood in several bowls and vases. Rose soon returned carrying a battered grip which she placed on the carpet next to the sofa. She went into the kitchen and returned with a bowl of boiling water. Without waiting for the doctor's instructions, she began to bathe and clean the wound before applying boiled comfrey leaves and binding it with a clean bandage.

'I picked up a lot from bein' with him,' she said, nodding at the prostrate doctor.

'How are you feelin'?' Trueman asked him. By way of reply Drummond grinned.

'It sure hurts, but I'll be OK.'

For the first time Rose seemed to take notice of Trueman.

'You're very welcome here,' she said. 'I know it's kinda late, but would you like a bite to eat?'

'Thanks, but I had somethin' before we set off.'

She looked closely at him. 'You look tired,' she said. 'I figure you could do with some rest.'

'You got that right,' Trueman replied.

'Me and Trueman have got things to discuss,' Drummond said.

'Whatever it is, it can wait till tomorrow. You need to rest too.' She turned back to Trueman. 'If you like, I can show you to your room.'

'I got to see to my horse,' Trueman said.

'Leave him to me. Come on upstairs.'

Trueman didn't argue. He sensed something resolute about the little woman and besides, she was quite right. He was feeling exhausted. The prospect of rest between clean sheets was welcome. He glanced at Drummond, but the man's eyes had already closed.

'Come on,' Rose urged. 'Don't worry about the horse or anythin' else.' She turned and he followed her up the stairs.

'What would you like for breakfast?' she asked. 'How does beef and baked beans with potato pancakes and sourdough bread sound?'

'Sounds real good,' Trueman said.

At the top of the stairs she turned to the right and opened a door.

'Here we are,' she said.

The room was small but comfortably furnished

with a bed, and a chest of drawers on which stood a bowl of water. A net curtain was partly drawn across a window through which Trueman could make out the shadowy contours of tree branches.

'It ain't much, but you're very welcome.'

'You don't know me,' Trueman said.

'Drummond owes his life to you. I reckon I know enough,' she replied. With a smile, she turned and left.

Trueman took off his boots and then sank down on the bed. He was feeling tired but his brain was racing, trying to piece together and make sense of the day's occurrences. It already seemed a long time since he had been riding along with little on his mind. Since then events had taken a new and decisive turn. He needed to accustom himself to his new circumstances. He needed to think about what to do next. From what Drummond had told him, he knew he was getting himself embroiled in a dangerous situation.

The odds were stacked against him if he went up against Kettle and his gang. And that was without taking Vogler into account – whoever he might be. If he hadn't stopped by the Dragon saloon, none of it might have been his concern. But when he recalled what had occurred there and how narrowly he had escaped with his life, he knew he couldn't just let the matter drop. The question was: what to do next? Before he had time to work that one out, his eyes closed and he slept.

CHAPTER TWO

Trueman awoke to find sunlight streaming through the gap in the curtains. It took a few moments for him to remember where he was, then he got to his feet and walked to the window. The stormy conditions of the previous night had gone and the sky was blue. His head felt clear. He washed himself with water from the pitcher and then made his way down the stairs. He smelt cooking and was greeted by Rose who put her head through the kitchen door.

'Good timin'. I thought I'd leave you to rest awhile.' Drummond was still lying on the sofa, covered with a blanket. 'I thought it best to leave him there,' she said. As if in response, the blankets stirred and Drummond raised his head.

'I reckon I could manage some of that cookin',' he remarked. Rose laughed.

'Seems like he's makin' a recovery,' she commented. She ducked back inside the kitchen and

Trueman took a seat next to the wounded man.

'Well, how are you feelin'?' he asked.

'Stiff and sore, but I'll be fine. Sorry I kinda flaked out last night. I hope you slept all right.'

'Like a baby,' Trueman replied. Good smells were wafting through the door.

'Wait till you've tasted Rose's cooking,' Drummond said.

Trueman soon found out that Drummond wasn't exaggerating. His plate was piled high and when he had finished Rose piled it up again. It was almost with a sense of relief that he finally wiped his plate clean and sat back to enjoy some steaming hot coffee.

'Ma'am,' he said, 'I ain't tasted anythin' so good in a long time.'

'I figure you boys needed somethin' solid inside you.' Rose made as if to begin clearing the table but Trueman got to his feet.

'Let me do that,' he said. She didn't demur and together they carried the plates to the kitchen. When they returned they found Drummond had got to his feet and was riffling through a drawer of the cabinet.

'What are you lookin' for?' Rose asked.

'I'm tryin' to find that old map of the trail through Salt Lake Desert.'

'You won't find it there. Wait a moment and I'll get it.' She went up the stairs and quickly returned with a rolled parchment.

'Here it is,' she said. 'You ain't looked at that map in a long time. What do you want it for?'

'Mr Trueman was askin' about Kettle and his boys.'

The reaction was instantaneous. Rose's shoulders straightened and she almost spat out the words.

'That varmint! It's about time . . .' She stopped and looked at Drummond. 'You ain't tellin' me it was some of Kettle's boys who did this to you?'

'Now quieten down, Rose. I don't know anythin' for certain.'

Rose grimaced. 'Don't try flannelin' me. We both know who it was.'

Drummond and Trueman exchanged glances.

'Let's sit at the table,' Drummond said. He spread out the map while Trueman and Rose looked on.

'There ain't a lot more to be said about Kettle,' Drummond said. 'Like I was sayin' before, I figure he's in the pay of someone else.'

'This man Vogler, you mean?'

'Yeah. That's if I've figured it out right. Kettle and his boys cover quite an area of territory. Dry Bluff is at the heart of it. Take a look at the map. As you can see, the wagon train route passes close by. It's the last real settlement before the wagons head into the wilderness. Just recently, the wagon trains have been comin' under attack. Some of 'em have even turned back.'

'But most have been gettin' through?'

'Yeah. The way I figure it, whoever's involved. . . .'

'Kettle, you mean?'

'Yeah: Kettle. He's makin' a good livin' out of it, but he's wise enough to realize that if he goes too far there could be repercussions.'

'What? From Vogler?'

Drummond grinned. 'You've hit the nail on the head there,' he said.

'So where does Vogler fit in?'

'A lot of the attacks on the wagon trains have been low-level thefts of cattle, oxen, horses. Sometimes it's more serious and people have been killed, but so far it's mostly small scale stuff. Those critters have got to end up somewhere and the way some folks figure it, they're bein' driven north to Vogler's ranch, the Buckle M.'

'Is that some distance away?' Trueman asked.

'Yeah, but if I'm right it's an indication of just how big the Buckle M seems to have become.'

Trueman thought for a moment.

'That's an awful lot of speculation,' he said, 'but not many facts. Why should there be a connection between Kettle and Vogler?'

'Well, for one thing, I've seen horses with a Buckle M brand in Dry Bluff. There was a bit of friction between some strangers and Kettle's men in the Dragon saloon and the name of the Buckle M came up. More particularly, I treated one man for a gunshot wound and he let drop a few hints about the link up between Kettle and the Buckle M. I agree it isn't much, but it fits.'

'Well,' Trueman said, 'I guess it's enough to go on.'

Drummond looked up at him. 'So, what do you plan on doin' next?' he asked.

Trueman thought for a moment. 'More to the point,' he said, 'What are you and Rose intendin'?'

'What do you mean? We ain't plannin' on doin' anything.'

'Maybe you'd better start.'

'I don't catch your drift.'

'Well,' Trueman said, 'don't you think you'll need to consider your own position. After all, you've just been shot by these varmints. You're lucky to survive. Maybe you won't be so lucky next time.'

'Next time?' Drummond said. 'Who says there's goin' to be a next time? Me and Rose have lived here a long time now and we're still survivin'.'

'They ain't just gonna leave it when they find out you're still around. Especially if they get round to makin' a connection between you and me.'

Drummond was about to argue when Rose cut in.

'Trueman's right,' she said. 'Things are different now.' There was a pause before she turned to Drummond.

'I think we'd better change your dressin's,' she

said. 'After that we can decide just what it is we're gonna do.' She went out and returned a few minutes later with some fresh bandages, with which she began to treat Drummond's wounded back.

'What about you?' Drummond said, addressing Trueman. 'You haven't said. You're welcome to stick round here.' He winced as Rose applied some iodine to his wound.

'That's a real nice offer but I got other plans.'

Drummond and Rose both looked at him expectantly.

'The way I see it, the only way you and any of the other folks around here are gonna be safe is if someone deals with Kettle.'

'You make it sound simple, but Kettle has upwards of a dozen men ridin' for him.'

'You say they use the Dragon saloon as their headquarters?'

'They do when they're around town, but they got other places.'

'There's a bunch of 'em in town right now and I figure there's a decent chance Kettle is amongst them. That's why I'm headin' right back for the Dragon saloon.'

'You can't do that. You'll be outgunned.'

'Last night they took me by surprise. This time I'll be ready.'

Rose had finished binding Drummond's wound. He pulled his shirt across his shoulder and looked up at Trueman.

'I'm comin' with you,' he said.

'No, you're not. Not even if you were fit. After what happened last night I kinda feel like dealin' with Kettle and his boys personally.'

Rose shook her head. 'I agree with Drummond. I think you're crazy. Just how do you propose goin' about dealin' with him?'

'What about the marshal? Doesn't he do anythin'?'

'Marshal Slick is more likely to take their side. You won't get any help from him.'

'Just so long as he don't get in my way, that's all I ask.' Trueman paused for a moment before continuing: 'And Kettle isn't the only one. From what you've told me, it seems that this man Vogler is the real problem.'

Rose and Drummond looked at him with shocked expressions.

'Now I know you're crazy,' Rose said.

Trueman was about ready to end the conversation, so he rose to his feet. Drummond struggled to stand up too but Trueman placed a hand on his shoulder to restrain him.

'Take it easy. As far as Kettle goes, leave him to me. But think about what I said. Even with Kettle out of the way, it might not be safe for you and Rose to stay here.'

Drummond was clearly not happy with the arrangement, but Rose seemed to take a different attitude. Having spoken her mind, she now appeared content to accept the matter.

'Let's do as Drummond suggests,' she said. She turned to him. 'Come back when you've done what you have to do.'

Trueman grinned and, getting to his feet, made his way towards the stairs.

'I'll get my guns,' he said.

It wasn't far to town and the sun was still quite high when Trueman arrived. In contrast to its drab and dismal appearance the previous evening, the place this time gave every appearance of normality. People walked up and down the boardwalks, passing in and out of the stores and emporiums. This time he was able to read the signs: *Harness Shop, Outfitting Supplies, Wagon Repairs*, all indicating the main business of the town supplying the needs of travellers. In several places a poster reading *Bull Whackers Wanted* indicated a shortage of drivers. Men rode by, some on horses and some on mules, while others congregated at street corners, a number of them still wearing the uniform of either the Northern or the Southern army.

Trueman rode on, but before he was in sight of his destination he dismounted and tied his horse to a hitch rack. Then, taking his rifle, a Sharps .50 buffalo gun, he continued on foot till he reached the Dragon saloon. He glanced around and observed that fewer horses were standing at the hitch-rail than had been there the previous night. He took a quick look at them. Most were unbranded but one carried the Buckle M brand. Once he had satisfied his curiosity, he stepped through the batwings.

The place was unexpectedly quiet. He guessed that since the outlaws had taken it over the regular townsfolk gave it a wide berth. Standing at the bar was a small knot of people among whom he was pleased to recognize most of his antagonists of the previous evening. He had barely set foot inside when voices rang out:

'Ain't that the fella from last night?'

'Hell, he's carryin' cholera!'

'Watch out, Swain!'

An atmosphere of panic began to spread rapidly as the gunnies leaped from their seats and made for the door. Trueman didn't hesitate but opened fire, blasting away at the ceiling. A chandelier came crashing down and some of the gunnies threw themselves to the floor. Swain spun round and his hand dropped towards his gun till he was confronted by the barrel of the rifle aimed straight at him.

'Throw your guns aside!' Trueman snapped.

Once the reverberation of his rifle fire had faded the place became unnaturally still. Swain hesitated for just a moment but a motion from Trueman's rifle was enough to make him respond.

Once he had given the lead, the others quickly followed suit.

'What is this?' Swain managed to say.

Trueman ignored the question, asking one of his own.

'Where's Kettle?'

For a moment the question hung in the air. Some of the men glanced at each other. Trueman squeezed the trigger of the rifle and the glass behind the bar shattered. The men standing there flinched. Trueman looked straight at Swain.

'Where's Kettle?' he repeated. The gunslick's eyes flickered in the direction of the stairs.

'Up there?' Trueman asked.

Without waiting for a reply he took a step forwards. Suddenly there was a roar of gunfire from up the stairs and bullets whined close by his head. The air was heavy with smoke and, taking advantage of the cover it provided, Trueman flung himself forward. He had a glimpse of legs on the stairs above him and he fired upwards. There was a howl of pain and a body came clattering down to the bottom. Without hesitation, Trueman stepped past the inert frame and ran pell-mell up the stairs. Reaching the landing, he saw an open door and sprinted for it.

At the same moment another figure appeared, staggering into the passageway. Trueman's finger was already on the trigger when he realized it was a woman. He brushed past her and sprang into the room. Another door leading to a balcony was open and he was just in time to see a man in the process of stepping over the rail. His instinct told him it was Kettle and he ran forward. The man was balanced on the ledge and, as Trueman approached, he jumped. There was a crash and a gasp of pain. When Trueman peered over he could see the man lying on his side, clutching at his leg.

'Hold it right there!' Trueman snapped.

Before Kettle could respond, Trueman heard footsteps behind him. Some of the gunslicks had reached the top of the stairs and were coming along the corridor. He stepped back into the room and, making his way to the doorway, let them have it with the buffalo gun. A couple of men at the front went reeling back. Then he flung the rifle aside and sprinted back to the balcony. Kettle had managed to get to his feet and was attempting to escape by staggering down the street. The boardwalks were deserted now, the people who had been walking near by having sought shelter. Trueman stepped over the rail and lowered himself to the street below. It was still quite a drop but he landed safely and was quickly on his feet in pursuit of Kettle.

The man limped along, glancing behind him, but it was obvious that he couldn't escape. In a last desperate bid for safety he staggered into the road, attempting to reach an alleyway on the other side just as a buckboard appeared, turning a corner. In other circumstances, Kettle might have made it but, impeded as he was by his injury, he was too slow. Frightened by his unexpected appearance, the lead horse reared and Kettle went down under its flailing hoofs. The buckboard rumbled on for a few more paces as its wheels went over Kettle's prostrate form before turning over in a tangle of broken shafts and harness. Coming alongside, Trueman stooped over Kettle's mangled body but it was obvious that he was dead. The driver, a young man, lay spread-eagled on the road but he was quickly on his feet.

Trueman glanced towards the Dragon saloon but there was no sign of any of the gunslicks. For a moment he thought of going back, but when his eyes saw the unmistakable figure of the marshal coming from the opposite direction he decided to call it a day. He had carried out his mission and it was unlikely that the gang of gunslingers would be able to recover from the loss of their leader; at least not for some time. He remembered what Drummond had said about the marshal and, taking advantage of the confusion, began to walk quickly away. He turned down the alley and then, following a route parallel to the main drag, quickly made his way back to where he had left his horse. With a last glance down towards the centre of town, he climbed into leather and rode away.

Once he was well clear of town he brought the

Steel Dust to a halt and dismounted. He sat with his back to a tree and rolled himself a smoke. He wanted a chance to think. It was clear enough that in eliminating Kettle he had only scratched the surface. From what Drummond had said, Kettle was only a minor figure, and there were others like him operating in the area. The chief figure behind it all appeared to be Vogler. In the long term, it was Vogler who needed to be dealt with. Vogler's ranch was apparently situated somewhere to the north, but where, exactly? He needed more information on Vogler, but where was he to find it?

Suddenly he thought back to the previous night, when he had seen the light on in the offices of the *Dry Bluff Epitaph*. Maybe the newspaper editor would be the man to supply it. It was worth a try. He took a last draw on his cigarette and was about to remount and return to Dry Bluff when he had a second thought. Things could be real hot for him back there. There was no sense in putting his neck on the line unnecessarily. No, this could be a job for Rose. Let things simmer down in town and then tomorrow she could pay a visit on the *Dry Bluff Epitaph*. It would be interesting to hear what she might have to say about how things were in town. There could be no doubt the events of that afternoon would have given the place a good shake-up.He flicked away the stub of his cigarette, climbed back into leather and continued on the trail back to Drummond's place.

*

The Buckle M lay basking in the late afternoon sunshine. It was situated in a beautiful spot, at the upper end of a long valley backed by low hills building up to the mountain ranges known locally as the Bear Wallows. There were plenty of places among those hills to conceal rustled cattle, while on the level ranges to the north and west the legitimate herds roamed free in large numbers. The ranch house itself stood alone. The bunkhouse, pens and corrals, together with other outbuildings, stood at a considerable distance away, concealed behind a screening stand of trees. The view was one to savour, but it was lost on the man who sat on the veranda observing it.

There was one simple reason for his discontent, and that was his failure so far to have acquired the neighbouring ranch: the Two Bar Cross. The owner himself was away somewhere back East. He had left his foreman in charge, a man named Fiske, and he was proving stubborn. So far he had resisted all the pressure Vogler had applied, but it was about time to take the gloves off.

Now, in addition to that, he had another issue to attend to. He had just been brought the news of a spot of trouble in Dry Bluff, involving the death of one of his operatives. Normally that would not have troubled him especially. Dry Bluff was a long way off and he wasn't sure that he even recalled the name of anyone called Kettle. It was a distraction he could have done without but he couldn't afford to ignore it. He had built up his empire on the basis of a ruthless attention to detail; he could not brook anything which might possibly be seen to threaten his authority. Once that aura of invincibility was dented, there was no knowing what it might lead to. The incident in Dry Bluff was nothing but a minor irritant, but it needed his attention.

He looked up at the approach of footsteps. It was one of his foremen, a man named Bigger, and one of the meanest gunslingers west of the Mississippi.

'What's the problem, boss?' the man said as he stood in front of the florid figure of Vogler. In a few words Vogler explained the situation.

'I don't want things to be left at a loose end,' he said. 'I expect Kettle's man – what's his name – yes, Swain, to take over operations down there, but that still leaves whoever was responsible. I don't intend him – whoever he is – to get away with it. That's why I want you to find out who he is and deal with him.'

'Sure thing, boss. Leave it to me,' Bigger said.

'You can start down there straightaway. Take a couple of the boys with you if you like. Don't waste any time. I'll expect to hear from you pretty soon.'

Bigger nodded, turned and walked away. It was a long ride but he was feeling pretty pleased. It was the sort of assignment he liked. The notches on his gun already told of the number of people he had eliminated when called upon to do so.

Standing on the veranda, Vogler watched him as he walked away. He remained in the same position when, presently, there was a sound of hoofbeats and Bigger came round the corner of the building riding a big buckskin. He drew up beside his boss.

'You needn't have any worries,' he said. 'Just leave this to me.'

'You ain't takin' anyone along with you?'

'Don't need anybody.'

Vogler looked closely at him. He wasn't sure he liked the man's attitude. He was too sure of himself by far. Still, he had been reliable in the past and hadn't given Vogler any reasons for doubting him.

'Take Micklum and Kenny,' he said, 'and make sure you don't let me down.'

Bigger nodded and touched the brim of his Stetson with his finger. Before much time had passed he and his two companions rode out of the yard and were presently lost to view in a cloud of dust.

When Rose arrived in town the morning after Trueman's escapade and stopped her buggy outside the newspaper offices, she couldn't help but notice a change in atmosphere. There was a buzz about the place, and from what Trueman had told her she guessed she knew the reason why. Even before she stepped down from the buggy the door opened and the proprietor himself emerged to greet her.

'Why, this is a pleasant surprise,' he said. 'Here, let me help you down.'

Rose had known Abe Thornton for a long time and there was warmth of understanding between them. He took her arm and they went through the door together. He led her into his room and she seated herself in a leather armchair next to his desk.

'Coffee?' he queried. It soon appeared and he sat down opposite her.

'I don't suppose you know about what happened here yesterday?' he asked. Rose knew perfectly well but she didn't say so.

'There was quite a shebang down at the Dragon saloon,' Thornton said. 'Someone apparently burst in and there was a shoot-out. In the course of it Kettle himself got killed. Some of his boys were shot and the rest have hightailed it out of town. It was as easy as that. The town is quietly celebrating.'

'Who was it?' Rose asked.

'Nobody seems to know. I've got my best reporter on the job right now.'

'Maybe it's a little early to start celebratin',' Rose said. 'Those outlaws might be back.'

'I don't think so. Even if they tried to rally I sense that things are different now. Folks were cowed. I reckon they won't let it happen the way it did again.'

There was a moment's silence while they finished their drinks, then Thornton took up the conversation.

'Anyway, what brings you to town? More especially, what brings you right here to the *Epitaph* offices?'

Rose was thoughtful for a moment.

'I guess it's kind of connected with what you've been tellin' me,' she resumed. 'I hope you're right about Kettle, but we both know there's more involved.'

'I've got someone looking into that too.'

'Then you'll probably have heard the name of Cush Vogler?'

Thornton gave her a searching look. His gaze was intense but in a moment it relaxed into a smile.

'Vogler,' he repeated. 'Yes, I have heard of him. In fact, if you remember, we had a conversation once before in which his name cropped up; you, me and Drummond. How is the old dog, by the way?'

'He's fine,' Rose said, without going into any of the recent events. Thornton's words had helped restore her equilibrium. He was right. The name had come up before.

'Tell me what you know about him,' she said.

'Now why would you be interested in Cush

Vogler?' Thornton asked. It was a rhetorical question, because he quickly went on: 'To be frank, I don't know a lot, but what I do know doesn't do him any favours. It seems he owns a big ranch north of here, somewhere in the foothills of the Bear Wallow range, near some township called Buzzard Roost. From what I can gather he didn't exactly acquire it by fair means. I wouldn't say it was common knowledge, but there's some folk suspect that he's the brains behind all the banditry that's been goin' on around these parts. I've made some enquiries and it seems that our friend Vogler has done time.'

'Really? On what charge?'

'Oh, pretty minor things. He was suspected of more serious offences but no one was able to pin those on him. The last time he came out of jail he disappeared from the map. It's only recently that he's re-emerged, always assumin' that the Vogler who owns the Buckle M is the same man.' When he had finished speaking Thornton got to his feet.

'Now you're here,' he said, 'let me show you the printing press in operation. I'm running a story on the Dragon saloon shoot-out right now. After that, why don't you and I go and have some lunch?'

'That sounds like a nice idea.'

He held out his hand and Rose took it. She would have liked to ask a few more questions about Vogler but she had probably gleaned as much information as she was going to get. Thornton had probably told her all he knew. She had learned a little more and, in particular, roughly where the Buckle M was situated. However, if there was anything else to learn, she might do so over lunch. In turn, she would have to be careful not to give away what she knew about Trueman.

CHAPTER THREE

A few days passed. Trueman was keen to be on the move but Drummond's injury needed time to heal, and after what had happened he was more than ever concerned about leaving his hosts. Besides, he wasn't averse to having an opportunity to relax and recuperate, enjoy the sunshine on Drummond's veranda and appreciate Rose's cooking. In truth, he had hardly been out of the saddle in a long time and he was more tired than he realized. One thing puzzled him. Drummond had explained why the outlaws had tried to kill him, but he hadn't explained the particular circumstances.

'What were you doing out there on the range?' Trueman asked. 'You were some way from Dry Bluff.'

'Yes,' Drummond replied. 'It happened like this. I was sitting on the veranda, just as we are now, when a rider came up. He explained he was with a wagon train that had recently passed through. There'd been an accident. Somebody's leg had got crushed. They didn't have a doctor with 'em. I couldn't very well say no.'

'You weren't set up?' Trueman asked.

'Nope, it was genuine. Seemed like a barrel fell on him. It wasn't as bad as it looked.'

'Then those varmints must have come across you by chance?'

'There are enough of 'em about. Maybe not so many now since you hit town.'

Trueman's eyes wandered across the garden and through the trees.

'You really never worry they might come out here?' he wondered.

'Nope. Leastways, not till now. I figure they weren't ever that concerned. They didn't like me, but killin' me wasn't one of their priorities. I guess when they came across me, they just took advantage of an opportunity.'

'Did you see who did it?'

'Nope. I was bushwhacked. I never saw it comin'.'

By the third day Drummond's wound had healed enough and Trueman had taken the decision to move on. So far, he had successfully avoided getting into a further discussion about Vogler, but it couldn't be avoided indefinitely. He was sitting with Drummond and Rose when, not for the first time, Drummond raised the question of what he intended doing next.

'Like we said before, you're welcome to stay on as long as you want,' Rose added. Trueman hesitated before replying.

'I've decided to head north,' he finally said.

'Head north?' Rose queried. Then she realized what he meant and she shook her head. Drummond was slower on the uptake.

'Lookin' to do some ranchin'?' he queried.

'Kind of,' Drummond replied.

'Drummond, you're an intelligent man, but I sometimes wonder about you,' Rose said.

Drummond looked at her in surprise. 'What do you mean?'

'Surely it's obvious, even to you. He's headin' north for the Buckle M.' It took another moment for Drummond to register what she was saying. Then he turned to Trueman.

'Vogler!' he exclaimed. 'Vogler! You're goin' up against Vogler.'

'Yup,' Trueman said. 'We discussed this before and we agreed that Vogler is the real problem, not Kettle. Since then, I've been givin' it some thought. If you take another look at that map of yours sometime, you'll see that Buzzard Roost, the place Thornton mentioned, is marked, like he said, just on the fringes of the Bear Wallow range. I'm aimin' to reach Buzzard Roost and then pick up any information I can. After that, I'll pose as a saddle tramp lookin' for work and ride on to the Buckle M.'

'You can't do that!' Drummond exclaimed. 'It would be far too risky. You'd probably be gunned down as soon as you set foot on Buckle M range.'

'I don't deny the risk,' Trueman said, 'but I've looked at the situation from all angles and it seems to me like it's the only way. Someone needs to be on the inside of Vogler's operations. Let's face it, at present all we've got to go on are rumours. We don't even know for sure that Vogler is the man we want.'

'I think we've got a pretty good idea,' Drummond replied.

'We need more than that. We need proof. We need to be sure that Vogler is responsible for all the trouble you tell me has been takin' place recently along the wagon train trail.'

'I figure he's responsible for more than that.'

'OK, but like I say, we need to be sure. And there' only one way to do that.'

Rose continued to shake her head, but after a few moments she suddenly turned to Trueman.

'I got a better idea,' she said.

'Yes? What?' Trueman replied.

'I see the sense of what you're saying,' she replied, 'but you don't have to put your head in a noose to find out what Vogler is up to. From what Thornton was tellin' me, it seems there's been trouble between the Buckle M and some of the other ranchers. So, instead of tryin' to find work on the Buckle M, why not try one of them? If Vogler has been leanin' on some of 'em, they might be findin' it hard to get enough hands to do the work.'

Trueman thought for a moment.

'Hell, why didn't I think of that?' he said. 'Now that you mention it, it seems quite obvious.'

'It certainly sounds like a better plan, but it's still very risky. In the last analysis, you'll be one man against Vogler's organization.'

'He might find there are other people ready to stand up to Vogler,' Rose suggested.

'I still don't like it,' Drummond said.

Trueman let the comment go unremarked. Instead, he returned to the subject of what Drummond and Rose intended doing.

'What about you two,' he said. 'Do you still mean to stay on here?' Rose and Drummond exchanged glances.

'As a matter of fact, we've been doin' some thinkin' too and we've come to a decision,' said Rose.

'Yes,' Drummond added. 'We've decided that if you're gonna ride for the Buckle M, we're comin' with you.'

Trueman was about to object when Rose spoke again.

'He's kiddin' you. Actually it's not a bad idea, but it ain't really what we've got in mind.'

'That's a relief,' Trueman said.

'No,' Drummond interjected, 'I think we're too long in the tooth for that sort of caper. But we ain't too old to up sticks and move. I guess we're gettin' a bit tired of this place and what you said about the danger from the gunslicks kinda clinched it. Although, after what you did, there's maybe no need to worry about them any more.'

'Clinched what?' Trueman said.

'We're movin' to Denver. We're gonna link up with the wagon train.'

It took a few seconds for Trueman to assimilate what Drummond and Rose were telling him. When it did, his face creased in a grin.

'Well,' he said, 'that was unexpected, but good for you. How long do you think it'll take to settle things up?'

'No time. We're just goin'.'

'We ain't sellin',' Rose said. 'Not till we know for sure whether we're comin' back or not. We know folks in town who'll keep an eye on the place. Somehow, though, I got a hankerin' for those Rocky Mountains.'

'In fact,' Drummond said, 'we're ridin' with you after all, leastways as far as that last wagon train that came through. I figure we should catch up with it before we've gone too far. Thanks to that incident with the barrel, they already know me.'

Trueman didn't know what to say; it was Rose who brought the discussion to a close.

'Well,' she said, 'I guess we can talk about all this

as we go. Right now, I figure we'd better get that old wagon ready to roll.'

After breakfast, Trueman saddled up for the ride. As he was tightening the girths on the Steel Dust, Drummond and Rose rolled up alongside him in the wagon.

'That didn't take you long,' he said.

'We already put in some provisions,' Drummond replied. 'We got one horse spare. Why don't you take it as a packhorse? You can take what you might need from us.'

Trueman laughed. 'Hell,' he said, 'I got to hand it to you folks. You sure don't waste any time. But you keep the extra horse. I figure you might need it more than me.' He stopped, suddenly more thoughtful. 'There's still time to change your minds,' he added.

'You've changed your tune,' Drummond said.

'With those gunslicks around, I was just tryin' to think what would be for the best,' Trueman replied.

'Now that's enough of that,' Rose cut in. 'Neither of us is likely to want to change our minds.' She looked down from the seat of the wagon at Trueman and then turned back to Drummond. 'Shall we show him?' she said. Drummond thought for a moment and then nodded.

'There's somethin' we'd like you to see,' Rose

said, turning to Trueman. 'Come with us.'

They both climbed down from the wagon and Trueman followed as they made their way round the side of the house and down through the orchard. When they had gone as far as the brook she turned and walked a little way along the bank. They came to some bushes and she parted them to reveal an overgrown grassy space in the middle of which was a stone marker leaning at a slight angle.

'Take a look,' Rose said.

Trueman walked to the stone and bent down. The letters were time-worn but he could still make out the legend:

Walter Drummond.
1838 – 1854

He took off his Stetson and stood up to find Rose next to him.

'Our boy,' she said. 'He was cut down by a gang of desperados.'

Trueman didn't reply but only nodded. Then he put his hat back on and they both moved to where Drummond had remained standing.

'I'm sorry,' Trueman said. 'Don't it make it harder to leave?'

'He ain't buried there. That's just a memorial.' Rose halted and Drummond took up the refrain.

'Assumin' we're right about Vogler, make sure you deal with him,' he said. 'I guess that's just one more reason.'

They turned away and made their way to the front of the house. Trueman had already observed the bond that seemed to exist between Drummond and Rose. Now he knew another reason why he was right in thinking that it was there.

They travelled steadily for the rest of the day, stopping every now and again to rest the horses and at one point crossing the wagon train's tracks. Apart from an occasional cabin, the country was deserted. When the sun began to dip over the edge of the horizon they found a suitable spot and set up camp. The night passed uneventfully but they found it difficult to sleep and before sunup they were up and about. They didn't waste much time over breakfast but soon set off again.

It was still early and they hadn't gone much further when they saw the wagon train. The wagons were drawn up in a circle, but there weren't the usual signs of preparation to move. The three of them sat and observed the scene for a few minutes. Just outside the circle a small group of people seemed to be involved in a heated discussion.

'What do you think?' Drummond said.

'Seems to me like somethin's not quite right.'

'They certainly ain't got too far,' Trueman commented.

'We'll soon enough find out,' Rose said.

Without more ado Drummond cracked his whip and the wagon rolled forward, Trueman riding alongside. As they approached, the disputants looked up and one of them drew his gun.

'No need for that,' Trueman said. 'We come as friends.' The man looked suspicious but put his gun back in its holster.

'Have you got some kind of problem?' Rose enquired.

'Yeah. Some of the oxen are missin'. Only twelve, but we can't afford to lose any. Looks like we had visitors during the night.' The man who spoke was obviously the wagon master. Trueman exchanged glances with his companions.

'We passed a cabin yesterday evening. It's the only habitation around. It might be worth payin' a visit.'

'What? You figure whoever rustled 'em might be there?'

'It's worth a try.' The wagon master looked at his companions. 'I've had some experience of these varmints,' Drummond added. 'I would suggest you don't let 'em get away with it.'

'What's it to you?' one of the men said.

'Let's just say we don't like rustlers,' Trueman replied. 'Besides, these folks have a real interest. In fact, they'd like to join the wagon train.'

'That's right,' Drummond said. 'How would you feel about havin' us along?' The wagon master looked them up and down, then nodded his head.

'Sure. The more the merrier. So long as you can pay your way.'

'We can pay,' Rose said.

The wagon master glanced at Trueman. 'Now that's settled,' he said to the others, 'what do you say to this gentleman's suggestion?'

The man who had drawn the gun looked unconvinced, but the others were less suspicious. Suddenly one of the men stepped forward and peered into Drummond's face.

'Hey, ain't you Doc Drummond?'

'Yes, I am,' Drummond replied.

'I thought I recognized you. You tended one of the drivers back in Dry Bluff. He dropped a barrel on his foot and crushed it.'

'How's he doin'?'

'He's fine, Doc. Still limpin' some, but he's OK.' The exchange served to settle any lingering suspicions and the atmosphere changed.

'What do you get out of this?' the man who had drawn his gun asked Trueman, echoing the wagon master's former question.

'A cup of coffee would be good.'

The man's expression, which had been grim, relaxed into a smile.

'You got it,' the wagon master intervened, then he turned to the others. 'Come on; let's do as the man says before the rest of the folk start gettin' nervous.' He looked at Trueman and his two companions riding the wagon. 'The name's Lawler. I'm the captain of the wagon train. Why don't you folks start movin' your wagon into line and introduce yourselves to some of the other folk?'

Drummond and Rose turned to Trueman. There was a moment of awkwardness but Trueman quickly broke the tension.

'I'll be back shortly,' he said, 'for that coffee.'

Rose smiled and Drummond nodded before pulling on the reins to urge the horses forward. As the wagon moved away, Lawler turned to address his men.

'OK,' he said, 'this is what I suggest we do. When we get to the cabin some of you take up a position overlooking it. I'll go right up to the cabin.'

'Mind if I come along with you?' Trueman said. 'It might be better if you weren't alone.'

Lawler looked at him. 'Of course not. In fact, if you've had experience of this kind of thing, you can do the talkin'.' He turned back to the others. 'If I touch my hat, you boys move pretty smart and surround that cabin. With any luck it might not come to shootin', but if it does, don't waste any of your lead.'

He didn't need to spell it out any further. The instructions were brief but understood and within an hour the men had taken up their positions. Leaving their horses under cover of a ridge, Lawler and Trueman started on foot for the cabin. It was a solidly built affair with an open corral containing a number of horses in its rear. As they approached,

Trueman pulled up his bandanna as the door of the cabin was flung open and three men appeared, one of whom he recognized as Swain. It was immediately apparent he was their leader, and Trueman thought he recognized one of the others from the Dragon saloon. It was clear that, despite what had happened, the remaining outlaws were still operating in the area. Trueman and the wagon master came to a halt.

'I want my oxen,' Trueman said.

Swain regarded Trueman with a questioning look. 'What's with that neckerchief?' he said.

Trueman didn't reply. Swain turned to his two companions with an ugly leer on his face before turning back to Trueman.

'What the hell have I got to do with any of your oxen?' he said.

'I ain't arguin'. Just deliver 'em. Twelve oxen.'

Swain's face turned red and he broke into a flurry of expletives. At the same moment another couple of men spilled out of the cabin.

'What's goin' on, Swain?' one of them said.

Swain ignored his question. 'Are you callin' me a thief?' he said to Trueman.

Without responding, Trueman glanced at Lawler, who gave the prearranged signal. The men who had been concealed behind the ridge came into view, walking down the slope leading to the cabin with their rifles raised. By the look on Swain's face it was quite obvious that he had been taken by surprise. His men looked anxiously at one another.

'As you can see, I mean business,' Trueman said. 'Two of your men may go beyond our lines and get the oxen. If anyone tries to follow, he will be shot. If those oxen are not delivered within the hour, we'll blow your cabin to hell and all of you with it if needs be. I know your type. Now, how does that strike you?'

Swain was finding it hard to restrain his fury but he saw that, for the moment at least, he was outfoxed. He turned and nodded to one of his men, the one Trueman thought he recognized, a small but wiry-looking individual who stepped forward to face him.

'Now just take it easy,' the man said. 'Seems to me like you're gettin' way too heated. Probably your oxen just strayed off. If you'd only calm down, maybe we could help you find 'em.' He peered closely at Trueman and Trueman wondered if he recognized him. It was unlikely, but if so, he didn't say anything.

'Twelve oxen,' Trueman repeated. 'All I'm askin' is that you give 'em back. The quicker you do it, the better. You've got two minutes to settle what you intend to do, but only two men can pass the lines.'

The wiry man looked at his leader.

'You've got it wrong,' Swain said. 'We ain't stolen nobody's stock. Like Krall says, seems like there's been some misunderstandin'. We're willin' to see if we can't find your oxen, but put down those rifles first.'

Lawler glanced at the men with the flicker of a smile playing about his lips. The others were looking calm and purposeful. Their Henry repeating rifles, recognizable by their brass mountings, remained levelled.

'Twelve oxen,' Trueman repeated.

Swain licked his lips. 'What do they look like?' he said.

'You bring me twelve good oxen,' Trueman replied. 'Whatever they look like, I reckon they'll be mine.'

Swain turned as if to go back inside the cabin.

'Wait right there,' Trueman said.

For a few moments silence hung heavy in the air. Then, from behind the cabin, two men emerged, leading horses. They mounted up and started riding. Lawler nodded at his men and at the signal they retreated a little way, then sat on the ground, prepared to wait as long as it took. It wasn't long. Presently the riders reappeared, driving the missing stock before them. Some of Lawler's men got to their feet, collected their horses and took over. They began to drive the oxen back towards the wagon train.

'Much obliged,' Trueman said.

He and Lawler turned and began to walk away. Once they had passed through their ranks, the rest of the men slowly retreated, rifles still trained on the cabin, till they were out of sight beyond the ridge. Then they mounted up and joined the others, drifting the cattle back towards camp. Lawler rode up close to Trueman.

'You figure it's over?' he queried. 'They ain't gonna like what just happened.'

'You got a long way to go and a heap of trouble ahead, but you won't have any more trouble from those varmints,' Trueman replied.

Lawler laughed. 'Well,' he said, 'I just hope you're right.'

'They're scum,' Trueman told him. 'Face up to 'em and they'll back down. But be prepared in any case.'

He didn't embellish his words because they were approaching the camp. Folks had been busy in their absence. Tents had been struck, oxen rounded up into teams, and items packed into the wagons, which were almost ready to roll. Lawler looked about with an air of satisfaction.

'I guess we got time for that coffee,' he said.

While final preparations for the journey were being made they were joined by Drummond and Rose as they made themselves comfortable over one of the remaining fires. Lawler was clearly pleased with the way things had gone but Trueman thought it wise to remind him to be careful.

'Don't worry,' Lawler said, 'we will be. We'd

already been warned about trouble along the trail, and I guess this just confirms it.'

'There could be other gangs operatin' further along the line,' Drummond said. 'The whole place is alive with the varmints just at the moment. It used to be the Sioux. They're still a threat but they've been quiet recently.'

'So where are you folks headed?' Lawler asked Drummond and Rose.

'Denver,' Rose said.

'That's fine. Denver is where we're headed,' Lawler replied. 'Thirty-five men, twenty-two women, twelve children, thirty-eight wagons. I guess that's thirty-six men, twenty-three women and thirty-nine wagons now. Oh, and thirty-eight revolvers and twenty-two guns. It isn't a large party, not like the old days. To be honest, I might not have taken it on at all except I got my own reasons for gettin' to the Rocky Mountains.'

He paused as a sudden thought struck him. 'Say, why don't you string along too, Trueman? You'd be right welcome.'

Trueman exchanged glances with Drummond and Rose.

'I'm headed north,' he said. For a moment he was tempted to elaborate but then thought better of it. He didn't want to get bogged down in explanations. Drummond seemed to sense his reluctance and broke into the conversation.

'Before we get movin',' he said, 'I figure it would

be a good idea if I took another look at that man's injured leg.'

He got to his feet. It was the signal for the others to do likewise. He made his way to one of the wagons, but soon returned.

'You're right,' he said. 'It's healin' up good.'

'We sure appreciate everythin' you folks have done for us,' Lawler said.

The wagon train was ready to move. Trueman, Drummond and Rose made their farewells before Trueman mounted up and rode away. When he had gone a little distance he turned to observe the wagon train.

Placing himself at the head of the column, Lawler gave the signal. The strident note of a trumpet rang out and slowly the leading division of wagons began to move. There was a cracking of whips and yells of encouragement to the animals from the teamsters who walked alongside them. Very precisely the scattered wagons formed an ordered line, each wagon taking its place in the procession, with Drummond and Rose's little wagon near the back, until the last one had rolled out of camp and the site was left churned up and deserted. Bringing up the rear and supplementing the oxen was a small remuda of horses.

As the wagons lumbered on Trueman was thinking that he was observing one of the last of its kind. He knew the days of the wagon train were almost over. The future lay with the railroads. He took a last glance at the wagons as they seemed to crawl across the grass, then turned his horse and commenced to ride.

When Bigger and his two gunslinging companions reached Dry Bluff they quickly established their headquarters in the Dragon saloon. If there was any sign of resentment on the part of any of Kettle's remaining gang, they were quickly subdued. Bigger's reputation had gone before him and his appearance confirmed the rumours. Those townsfolk who saw the trio ride in were immediately fearful. They had lived with Kettle for long enough to recognize the type and there was little doubt in their minds that an even worse regime was about to be imposed upon them. The period of calm they had enjoyed since Trueman dealt with Kettle and his outlaw gang had proved of short duration. For his part, Bigger very soon decided what he needed to do following what had happened to Kettle. It was Dungan who supplied him with the information he needed.

'I don't know who was involved, but I figure it might be worth havin' a word with Doc Drummond.'

'Who in hell is Doc Drummond?'

'An interferin' polecat is what he is. He has a place a little way out of town he shares with an old squaw woman.'

'That's all very interestin' but what has it got to

do with what happened to Kettle?'

'That varmint who came back and did the shootin' had us fooled with the cholera story, but when he rode away that first night I managed to get a glimpse of the man he was carryin' on his horse. I thought I recognized him but I wasn't sure at the time. Afterwards I figured it was Doc Drummond. Later I heard he'd been shot by some of our boys. That seemed to confirm it.'

There was an exasperated look on Bigger's face. 'Hell, I reckon you coyotes deserve everythin' you got. Can you not even shoot straight?' Dungan did not reply and after a moment's pause, Bigger turned to his two companions.

'Well, what do you say, boys?' he asked. 'I reckon we should pay a call on this Doc Drummond *hombre.* Dungan, get saddled up. You can show us the way.' Dungan nodded and started to move but he was brought to a halt as Bigger spoke again.

'By the way,' he said, 'I'll be wantin' to have words with Swain. Where did you say he was?'

'He's taken off with some of the boys. He was figurin' to pay a visit on a wagon train that's just passed through.'

Bigger considered Dungan's words for a few moments but didn't seem to come to any conclusions. Instead, he smiled and turned to the bartender.

'Set 'em up,' he said. 'Drinks all round, and then it's down to business.'

*

Trueman woke with a start. Instinctively reaching for his gun he sat up and listened closely. The night was filled with a great silence but he trusted his instincts and knew something or somebody was out there. Quickly he got to his feet and rearranged his tumbled blanket. He moved across to where the Steel Dust was tethered and took his rifle from its scabbard. Then he slipped into the shelter of the trees. He listened closely for any sounds and after a time thought he heard the distant drumming of approaching horses. There was little doubt in his mind as to who it was: Swain and his gang.

He peered through the bushes. The last faint embers of the fire cast an eerie glow over the clearing, where his blanket suggested the outline of a sleeping figure. He continued to listen, but despite his best efforts he could distinguish nothing further. Briefly, he was puzzled by this till the obvious answer suggested itself. Swain would not want to alert him. He would ride as far as he thought was safe, then advance the rest of the way on foot, anticipating catching him by surprise.

The breeze rustled through the bushes and the starlight created patches of illumination among the shadows. Despite the approach of the gunslicks, Trueman felt calm. He knew what he had to do. The minutes crept by and seemed to extend into hours, but still nothing happened. Then, when Trueman was beginning to wonder whether he might be wrong after all, he heard the Steel Dust snort and stamp. He drew back slightly further into the shelter of the bushes and raised his rifle in readiness.

Although he was prepared for action, what happened next was unexpected. Suddenly the silence was riven by a tremendous explosion of noise that was almost deafening. Stabs of flame blossomed in the darkness like exotic flowers, and bullets whined and sang like a demonic choir, ripping into the empty blanket where he had been sleeping. The savage burst of gunfire seemed to go on and on and the open space where he had set up camp was hidden behind a dense pall of smoke, which hung like a ghostly curtain. A long time seemed to pass before the noise reached its climax and then it abruptly stopped. In the sudden silence his ears were ringing. He licked his lips. Whether he came out of the situation alive depended almost entirely on what happened next.

He didn't have long to wait. The smoke had just begun to clear when a couple of figures appeared in the open, quickly followed by a third. Still Trueman waited, counting the number of arrivals. Very quickly the open space was occupied by a number of figures, all carrying rifles. He held on for a few moments more till he was satisfied that no one else was left. The leading figure moved towards his blanket and, levelling his rifle, began to pump lead into what he thought was Trueman's sleeping form. Trueman let him carry on for a few more moments, then he raised his rifle and opened fire. The man spun round, his gun still blazing, but into the air, then he fell backwards into the fire. There was instant pandemonium as several more gunslicks collapsed and others began to run.

They didn't get far. Two or three of them turned to return fire, but their shooting was wild. Their bullets cut through the bushes and whined uncomfortably close by as Trueman ducked low in order to make himself less of a target. The gunnies were confused and disoriented, however, and more of them crumbled beneath Trueman's fire.

Because of the smoke it was difficult for Trueman to make out what was happening. He was suddenly confronted by a looming figure, who came towards the bushes with both barrels of his gun blazing. A bullet grazed Trueman's cheek and he dropped on one knee, firing upwards as he did so. The man stopped and spun round before collapsing into the bushes close by. There was a lull in the fire and Trueman could now see that the clearing was deserted apart from the corpses of those gunslingers who had fallen. He had no way of knowing how many of them there were, but he had a shrewd suspicion that not many of them could have escaped. They had paid the price of their carelessness.

A palpable silence now replaced the shattering din and nothing moved behind the veil of smoke. Still Trueman waited till he was satisfied that it was safe to emerge from cover. As he was about to do so, he caught the sound of horses' hoofs, which quickly faded away into the night. With a last glance around he stepped forward and almost tripped over the outflung arm of the man who had rushed him. He glanced down, then looked closer at the features of the dead gunslinger. They were those of the man who had accosted him that first night. What was the name the others had called him? He remembered it now: Swain. He stood upright again and, moving into the open, surveyed the scene of carnage. In addition to Swain, three of the outlaws lay dead and, looking a little further afield, he saw two others. He stood for some moments in thought. The night was almost gone and the cold breath of dawn chilled the atmosphere. From somewhere he heard the whinny of one of the horses his attackers had left behind. They had come looking for him in numbers, and it was going to take some time to bury them.

CHAPTER FOUR

Bigger, Micklum and Kenny, led by Dungan, drew their horses to a halt outside Drummond's house and took a few moments to look around.

'Looks to me like there ain't nobody at home,' Kenny said.

By way of reply Bigger drew his six-gun and fired some shots, which shattered the windows and sent the echoes flying. A scattering of birds rose into the air from the trees behind the house, cawing and wheeling. All four riders dismounted and clattered their way up the path to the veranda. Bigger stepped on to the porch and pulled at the door. It was locked. He swung his boot and the wood splintered. The others joined in and the door finally yielded under the impact. As it sagged on its hinges they burst into the room.

'Drummond, are you there?' Bigger yelled. When there was no response he turned to the others. 'Take a look around here. I'll check upstairs.'

It didn't take long for them to search the house and when they had done so they made their way down through the orchard, spreading out as they did so. Bigger knew there was small chance of their finding Drummond or anybody else, but as he turned to make his way back he heard Dungan's high-pitched voice call out:

'Over here! I've found somethin'.' He made his way over to where Dungan was kneeling in the grass.

'What is it?' he said.

'Sign. Look, there are clear traces of a wagon.' Bigger leaned over. The marks of the wheels were evident even to him.

'I reckon there was someone ridin' a horse too,' Dungan said. He got to his feet and walked away, looking closely at the ground. Presently he stopped and glanced back.

'Yes, I'm right. Take a look over here. There are horse-droppings.'

Bigger took another look and then turned to Dungan.

'You say Drummond lives here with his woman?'

'Yeah.'

'Well, it looks like they decided to leave.'

'Maybe he just took the wagon into town?'

'I doubt it,' Bigger said. 'The way I see it, they've lit out altogether. And I reckon that varmint Trueman is the one on the horse.' He thought for a moment. 'You say you know somethin' about trackin'. Do you figure you could follow the trail?'

'It shouldn't be too hard to follow those wagon tracks. They're fairly fresh, too. They can't be too far ahead of us.'

'That's good enough. Boys, I figure we know what to do next.'

'Hunt 'em down?' Micklum suggested.

'Right. But first there's another bit of business we need to attend to.' The others looked at him with puzzled expressions on their faces.

'Burn this place down,' Bigger said. It took a moment for his words to register with them, but when they did Kenny gave out a whoop.

'Let's do it,' Micklum yelled. They ran to the front of the building and made their way back inside.

'This is sure gonna be fun!' Kenny commented.

It was a testimony to the fact that they had done this type of thing before that in no time at all smoke began to pour from the building. They emerged into the open as the first tongues of fire spread rapidly from one room to the other.

'Mount up, boys!' Bigger ordered.

They rode a little distance, then stopped to watch the conflagration. The building was now a raging inferno of fire and even at a distance the heat hit them like a wall. The crackling of the flames was like the hissing of a myriad snakes as a pillar of fire burst through the roof, sending a shower of sparks into the air. The roar of the flames was accompanied by their own whoops of delight.

'That's part payment for what Drummond did back in Dry Bluff,' Bigger said.

'It was Trueman who caused all the trouble,' Dungan commented.

'It makes no difference. Trueman, Drummond, whoever else is involved, they're gonna regret ever tryin' to cross Vogler.'

Dungan thought regretfully for just a moment of his old boss, Kettle. It seemed he himself didn't account for much in the scheme of things, but he knew where his own best interests lay. It would pay him to give his allegiance to Bigger. Right now that meant putting his tracking skills to the test; he had confidence in his ability. With a last glance at the sagging wooden skeleton bathed in flames which had once been Drummond's and Rose's house, he turned and rode away.

Trueman had been riding steadily across a landscape that was high, rolling and arid, with barely a shrub visible to relieve the monotony, when he saw ahead of him a line of hills and he knew he was nearing his destination. The hills were quite low but in places rose higher, their slopes covered with cedars and small shrubs. The ground descended towards a slow-moving stream across which he splashed his horse, bringing it to a halt on the opposite side. Drummond had given him the map and now he pulled it from his shirt pocket to take another look.

Buzzard Roost was marked, but the map wasn't very detailed. It gave him some sense of the direction to follow, which took him parallel to the line of hills. He kept riding till eventually he rounded a projecting shoulder of rock and saw ahead of him, nestling close to the hills down which flowed a thin trickle of water, a few scattered cabins with some taller frame buildings in the centre.

Well, he thought, *I guess this is it.*

The place could hardly be called a town but it boasted a saloon. Trueman drew his horse to a halt outside it and stepped out of leather. Three horses were tethered at the hitch rail and he looked at their brands. None of them was a Buckle M. It had been a long shot but he felt slightly disappointed. He turned away and stepped through the batwing doors.

As he made his way to the bar Trueman's eyes quickly took in the scene. The place was quiet. A few people sat at tables and one man stood alone at the bar. The bartender glanced up idly at his approach.

'What have you got?' Trueman asked.

'Whiskey. Beer.'

'Make it a beer,' Trueman said. The bartender reached for a bottle and began to pour.

'Travelled far?' he queried. 'We don't get a lot of visitors around these parts.'

'Passin' through,' Trueman replied.

The bartender set the drink on the bar in front of Trueman and stepped away. He didn't seem to be interested in pursuing the conversation, but the man standing by the bar unexpectedly took up the theme.

'You're on a trail to nowhere,' he said. 'There's nothin' much here.' Trueman turned to face him.

'I heard there are a few ranches,' he said.

'Yeah, that's true.' The man seemed to consider Trueman's statement.

'I'm lookin' for work,' Trueman continued. 'You wouldn't know if there's any rancher could use an extra hand?'

'You done ranch work before?' the man asked.

'Sure. I ain't got any references with me, though, if that's what you're askin'.' The man looked at him for a moment, then his face broke into a grin.

'You might just be in luck,' he said. 'I work for an outfit called the Two Bar Cross.'

'It's owned by a man called Crosby,' the bartender interrupted. He stopped and looked slightly sheepish before concluding lamely: 'He's a friend of mine.'

The man gave him a long, hard look which Trueman couldn't interpret.

'I'm the foreman,' he continued after a moment. 'The name's Fiske.' Trueman responded with his own name.

'OK, Trueman. If you like, you could ride over. It might not be down to me in the long run, but I could sure use an experienced hand right now.'

'Sounds like a decent offer,' Trueman said. He was thinking hard. Things seemed to be falling into his lap, but was there a catch?

'Why don't you think it over?' the man said. 'Right now, I've got to be movin', but if you decide to ride over to the Two Bar Cross you can't go far wrong. Just take the trail west out of Buzzard Roost and keep ridin' till you reach a fork. Take the side trail and presently you'll see a sign for the Two Bar Cross.'

'I can give you more details if you need 'em,' the bartender said.

'That'll be fine,' Trueman replied.

'OK,' Fiske said. He touched the rim of his Stetson. 'Be seein' you folks.' He turned and walked away, his spurs clinking on the sanded floor of the saloon. The batwings swung to behind him and then the sound of horse's hoofs announced his departure.

'You could do a lot worse than work for the Two Bar,' the barman said. 'Fiske is a good man.'

Trueman took his beer and sat down at a corner table. Things were working out better than he could have expected, but again he wondered: was he doing too well? When he had checked the horses before entering the saloon, one of them had carried a Two Bar Cross brand. That seemed to prove Fiske's credentials. He finished his drink, got to his feet and made his way to the bar.

'Yeah? Can I get you anything else?' the barman queried. Trueman ran his hand across his stubbled chin.

'Is there somewhere a man can get a shave and a bath?' he asked. The barman grinned.

'Sure,' he replied. 'Right across the street.'

'Thanks,' Trueman said. He turned and made his way to the batwings.

After some initial success in following the sign left by Trueman and his party, Dungan was beginning to realize the limits of his tracking skills. Much to Bigger's annoyance, he was finding it difficult to follow the trail. He rode with his eyes searching the ground and there were frequent halts as he slid from the saddle to examine the ground more closely.

'I thought you said you could do this,' Bigger snapped.

Although he couldn't really tell for certain which way their quarry had gone, Dungan thought it diplomatic to pacify Bigger by pretending that he did.

'Looks like they kept goin' in this direction,' he said. He was about to mount up once more when Bigger held up his hand and reached for his field glasses.

'What is it?' Micklum asked.

'Looks like a couple of riders. They're comin' on pretty fast.' Bigger and his two companions drew their rifles from their scabbards while Dungan climbed back into leather.

'Let me take a look,' he said. Bigger handed him the glasses and he clapped them to his eyes. After a few moments he let out a low whistle.

'I recognize them,' he said. 'They were with Swain when he set off to attack the wagon train.'

'Then what the hell are they doin' now?' Bigger wondered. They didn't have long to wait as the two riders came up, bringing their horses to a sudden halt.

'Dungan!' one of them said, recognizing the would-be tracker. Dungan nodded in response.

'Howdy, Krall,' he said.

The newcomers looked at Bigger and his henchmen. Something about them made them nervous.

'Where's Swain and the rest of the boys?' Dungan asked.

The two men exchanged glances, licking their lips before answering: 'They're dead.'

Bigger sheathed his rifle. 'I think you'd better explain,' he said. Haltingly, the two riders explained about the attack on Trueman's camp.

'Once we got away we headed back to the cabin, but we didn't know what to do next. We figured the best thing would be to return to Dry Bluff.'

Bigger had listened to their tale with growing

impatience. When they had finished he drew his six-gun and pointed it menacingly, first at one and then at the other.

'You no-good pair of skunks,' he hissed. 'I ought to shoot you both.'

'It wasn't our fault. We were tricked.'

'You'd have done better to keep on ridin'.' For a few moments more it looked like Bigger might carry out his threat, but then he put the gun back in its holster.

'I'll give you another chance,' he said. 'We're lookin' for a varmint named Trueman. He's almost certainly the man who shot up your party. You'd better show us where this all happened. We should be able to pick up his trail from there.'

'Trueman!' Krall gasped. His thoughts went back to the masked man who had shown up demanding the return of the stolen oxen. Him again!

'Sure,' the other man said. 'We'd be mighty glad to help.'

Bigger gave them a searching look. 'You'd better not let me down,' he said. He seemed lost in thought for a moment; then when he spoke it was almost as if he was talking to himself.

'This little enterprise seems to be takin' a mite longer than I thought. But there are more than enough of us to deal with Trueman.'

'He's a tricky customer,' Krall hissed.

'You boys might not be able to handle him,'

Bigger said. Krall shrank back, realizing he might have been pushing his luck. Bigger ejected a stream of saliva over his horse's head.

'OK,' he concluded. 'We're wastin' time. 'Let's ride.' Digging his spurs into his horse's flanks, he set off. The others followed in his wake.

It was quite late in the day when Trueman set off for the Two Bar Cross. He wasn't expecting to ride far, but if it took longer than he reckoned he was happy to camp out for the night. Presently he reached a fork and, guessing it was the one which Fiske had told him would lead to the ranch, he took it. The country was mostly open graze but as he rode the trail began to climb upwards in the direction of the hills.

He was going at a steady pace, not thinking of much, when suddenly there was a loud bang and fragments of hard leather struck him in the face as a bullet slammed into his saddle horn. He smelled burning as the Steel Dust reared, hoofs flailing. He dropped the reins and as he desperately sought to regain control and stop the animal from going over, he toppled sideways from the saddle. He landed awkwardly, banging his head hard on the ground; it took him a few moments to struggle to his feet. His shoulder and head hurt and blood was flowing from the impact of the leather shards from his saddle horn. Through the ringing in his ears he heard the sound of hoofs and looked up to see a trio of riders. A voice rang out:

'Don't move. Drop your gunbelt!'

For a moment he considered going for his gun but he quickly saw that it would be pointless. Reluctantly he complied. He looked up and saw that the voice belonged to a mean-looking individual with a drooping moustache and long hair that hung almost down to his shoulders. His two companions swung down from their saddles and came up close.

'Now, you'd better explain just what you're doin' on private property,' the man snapped.

'I didn't see any sign. How was I supposed to know I'm on claimed land?'

'This is Buckle M range. We don't take kindly to trespassers.'

Trueman was about to offer an account of his meeting with Fiske when he found himself staring into the barrel of the man's rifle.

'We're gonna show you how we deal with trespassers,' he snarled.

'Now look here,' Trueman began, but he didn't get any further as the man's two companions suddenly seized him by the shoulders. One of them twisted his arms behind his back. Their leader dismounted and approached him. Without any warning, he swung his rifle butt and brought it crashing into Trueman's stomach. Trueman doubled up and would have fallen had the other two not held him upright. He felt nauseous and tried to brace himself for the next assault but there was nothing he could do to protect himself as the man, abandoning the rifle, aimed a savage blow with his fist at Trueman's jaw. Trueman's head snapped back and then, through a cloud of darkness which was beginning to gather at the corners of his vision, he heard another voice exclaim:

'Stop that right now! Move away from that man. And don't try anythin' or I'll shoot you where you stand.'

In response to the man's command the two who had been supporting Trueman's weight stepped away, dumping him unceremoniously on the ground.

'Get back on your horses and get the hell out of here,' the voice boomed.

Trueman gathered up his last reserves of grit and determination to look up in the direction of the newcomer. He recognized him at once. It was Fiske and he was sitting astride a big roan stallion. The two who had been holding him climbed back into leather but their leader stood his ground.

'We found him trespassin' on Buckle M property. He needed a warnin'.'

'You know this isn't Buckle M land. And I know who you are. You're Drago Strangholt. I recognize your type and you don't scare me. Now get goin', the three of you, and count yourselves lucky I didn't shoot you.'

The long-haired man made to retrieve his rifle,

which he had dropped to the ground in order to beat Trueman with his fists, but the response from Fiske was immediate. A shot rang out and the man leaped back as a plume of earth shot into the air near where his rifle lay.

'Leave it! The next shot will be for you.'

The man hesitated for just a moment longer, staring at Fiske with twisted features. After some moments he turned away and mounted his horse. With a curse he dug his spurs into its flanks, then all three of them turned and rode away. Fiske watched them till they were gone. Dropping from his horse, he moved to where Trueman was kneeling.

'I'm sorry about what just happened,' he said. 'Here, let me take a look. Looks like you've taken quite a beating.'

'I figure you got here in the nick of time,' Trueman managed to say. Fighting back the inclination to retch, with Fiske's assistance he succeeded in struggling to his feet. 'What the hell was that all about?' he gasped.

'I feel real bad. Maybe I should have realized . . .' Fiske broke off. 'Here, sit down on this rock. Try and take it easy. I'll go get your horse. There's a line cabin not far from here. When you think you might be able to ride we'll head for it and you can be patched up. There'll be time enough to explain things then.'

*

Cush Vogler had just settled down to look at some accounts when there was a knock on the door.

'Come on in,' he shouted. He wasn't in the best of moods. The situation with regard to the Two Bar Cross was causing him increasing irritation and, on top of that, the stream of wagon trains heading West had dried to a trickle. Robbing them had provided a steady source of income, but so far as they were concerned he could see the writing on the wall. Some of his men were getting restless. They needed something to keep them occupied. He laid aside the paper he had been looking at as the door opened to admit Drago Strangholt.

'What is it now?' he asked. Strangholt did not venture into the room but stood by the door.

'Me and the boys thought you should know that there's been some trouble involvin' Fiske.'

'Fiske?' Vogler queried. 'The foreman of the Two Bar Cross?'

'Yeah, that's him. We caught some varmint close to Buckle M range. We were teachin' him the usual lesson when Fiske came by and put a stop to it.'

'Couldn't you have dealt with it? Hell, he's only one man.'

'He got the drop on us. There was nothin' we could do.'

'So why are you tellin' me this?'

'I figured it was somethin' you ought to know, is all.' Vogler let out a sigh. He was feeling exasperated.

'OK,' he said. 'I get the picture. Go back to the bunkhouse and leave it with me.'

Strangholt grunted something inaudible in reply and made his way out of the door. When he had gone Vogler remained sitting at his desk, thinking about what he had just heard. Although he resented Strangholt's intrusion on his time and privacy, part of him had to acknowledge that Strangholt was right to draw his attention to it. Fiske was becoming more than a nuisance. Maybe it was time now to deal with the Two Bar Cross – and with Fiske in the process. His men needed an outlet for their pent up energies. They were out of reach of the law. It would be easy enough to put Fiske and his cowboys out of business once and for all and add the Two Bar Cross to his growing empire. The trouble was, most of his hired guns knew little or nothing about ranching. He was already stretched. It was something else that needed thinking about.

It took a little while for Bigger to realize the fact but, after following Trueman for some time, it became obvious even to him that they were heading back in the direction of the Buckle M. Maybe it was just a coincidence, or maybe there was more to it.

After his initial problems Dungan seemed to grow into his task, following the sign left by Trueman with greater ease the longer the pursuit continued, mainly through the assistance of Krall, who seemed to know something about tracking. In addition to the usual indications left by the horses, they also found traces of where Trueman had camped. It was when the foothills of the Bear Wallow range came into sight and the trail led towards Buzzard Roost that Bigger began to get excited. Chances were that he would catch up with his quarry there and he relished the prospect.

As he rode with his party down what passed as the main street of the settlement, people who were on the street looked on with concern because they had reason to recognize his type. Since Vogler had moved into the area after acquiring the Buckle M things had not been the same. It didn't take them long to realize that most of the men who rode for him were not the usual type of ranch hand. There was no doubting that they were men who relied not on their range skills, but on their expertise with the gun. It was true that the number of real incidents had been few, but every time any of the Buckle M riders came into town there was tension in the air. People were cowed and on edge. There was a feeling that some day the tension would erupt in genuine violence.

They watched as Vogler rapidly acquired more territory, usually by taking over local businesses and enterprises by means they knew were crooked. The area was largely unspoiled; without decent folks to help develop it it was in danger of becoming a lawless backwater. Some people questioned what Vogler was doing here at all. The fact that he had chosen to set up the Buckle M in the foothills of the Bear Wallow range was something of a mystery. It suggested that perhaps he had something to hide.

When they arrived at the saloon Bigger and his companions dropped from the saddle, fastened their horses to the hitch rack and pushed their way inside. The barman looked up at their approach and licked his lips. His throat suddenly felt dry. He recognized Bigger, but even if he had never seen him before he would have known what to expect. Bigger stood at the bar and put his foot on the rail while his companions lined up alongside him.

'Whiskey!' Bigger rapped.

The barman reached for a bottle and began to pour. When the glasses were filled he made to put the bottle back but Bigger laid a restraining hand on his arm.

'Leave the bottle,' he said. He looked close and hard at the barman. 'Your name's Morrison, ain't it?'

The barman nodded. Bigger didn't follow up his statement but left it to hang in the air like a threat as he and his companions downed their whiskeys and then indicated for the barman to refill their glasses. Bigger turned his head and looked around the saloon. The place had emptied somewhat since his arrival but a few hard drinkers still sat at the tables.

'Say,' Bigger exclaimed, 'what sort of a place is this anyway? Me and the boys have been ridin' for a long time. Where are the cards? Where are the girls? Hell, there ain't even a piano.'

The barman shuffled awkwardly: 'I'm sorry, there's not much call—' he began, but quickly broke off as he found himself looking into the barrel of Bigger's gun.

'Then it looks like we're gonna have to provide our own entertainment.'

'I don't understand—'

The barman's words were again cut short as Bigger squeezed the trigger and a bullet whistled past his ear to smash into the mirror behind the bar. The reverberations of the shot echoed round the room to be followed by a deep silence.

It was short-lived. At a signal from Bigger, his companions drew their shooters and, to an accompaniment of whoops and cries, began to fire at random. The remaining customers flung themselves to the floor as bullets whined and ricocheted around the room. Plaster fell from the walls and ceiling, shards and splinters of wood flew into the air and glass shattered as the bottles behind the bar exploded. The shooting reached a climax as the room filled with a thick pall of smoke. As the fusillade came to a halt, the laughter of Bigger's men echoed round the room. Only one man had not taken part, and that was Krall, not because of any scruple, but because he had been more interested in the whiskey.

The barman, who had been cowering behind the counter, rose slowly to his feet and stood trembling in front of the broken remnants of his bar. Blood flowed from a deep cut above his eye where he had been hit by a flying splinter of glass, but he scarcely noticed it. Bigger took a final swallow of his drink and turned as if to go, but immediately turned back to the barman.

'Oh, by the way,' he said. 'I'm lookin' for a man called Trueman. He's ridin' a Steel Dust mare. I have reason to think he might have been this way recently.'

The barman hesitated, uncertain how to react, but when Bigger's hand moved towards his gun he quickly decided that this was a time when discretion was the better part of valour.

'He was in here,' he said. 'Leastways, I think that was the name.'

'When was this?'

'Just the day before yesterday.'

'Where is he now?'

'I don't know. I think . . .' Bigger's gun was back in his hand and pointing at the bartender. 'He got talkin' to a fella called Fiske.'

'What! Not the same Fiske who's runnin' the Two Bar Cross?'

'I think that's him,' the bartender said. 'Fiske said he might have a job for him.' Bigger stared hard at the hapless barman and then spat into the sawdust.

'You'd better be tellin' me the truth,' he said.

'Honest, I'm tellin' you what I know.'

'You ain't holdin' anythin' back?'

The barman shook his head. Beads of sweat had gathered on his brow and ran into the blood coursing down his cheek. Bigger stood immobile, as if considering what to do next.

'The Two Bar Cross,' he hissed. 'They're gonna get what's comin' to them.'

His face was twisted with rage and the tension in the atmosphere was palpable. For a few more moments the outcome was uncertain, then he suddenly put his gun back in its holster. After ejecting a stream of saliva in the direction of the cuspidor, he turned and made his way to the batwings, followed by his companions. The batwings swung to behind him and the barman seemed as if he would sink to the floor. He was trembling and clutched at the rim of the bar for support. The few customers who had remained got up from the floor and stared at the batwings through which the sound of hoofs told them the gunslicks had left, leaving a cloud of dust in their wake. They looked at one another wordlessly before surveying the wreckage of the saloon, thankful that at least they were still alive.

CHAPTER FIVE

Trueman opened his eyes. He was lying on a bunk, covered with a blanket, but when he tried to sit up to look around he quickly sank back with a gasp of pain. His head hurt and he felt confused, but after a few moments he remembered what had happened to him. More cautiously he began to raise himself upright again, and this time succeeded. He sat on the edge of the bunk and looked around. He was in a small cabin, almost bare of furniture except for a rough table, a couple of chairs and some empty shelves. Sunlight was streaming through a window devoid of curtains and through it he could see the outline of hills.

Very gingerly, he swung his feet to the floor and stood up. His midriff felt sore, and when he opened his shirt to take a look he saw that it was badly bruised and that someone had made an attempt to treat it: a poultice was held in place by a rough bandage which had become loose. A shard of glass on the wall served as a mirror and when he glanced at his face, he saw that it was also cut and bruised. His gunbelt hung from the back of one of the chairs; he was about to fasten it on when the door opened and Fiske entered.

'You shouldn't be movin' about,' he said. 'Get back on the bed and take it easy.'

'I'll be OK,' Trueman replied.

'I was out feedin' the horses,' Fiske told him. 'Here, take this while I rustle up some breakfast.' He held out a flask from which Trueman took a long swig. When he had finished his face creased up in a grimace and he shook his head.

'Hell,' he said. 'What is that stuff?'

'Rotgut, but I figure it might do you some good.' Trueman grinned and took another sip.

'I reckon you could have a point,' he said.

'How does bacon and beans sound?'

Again Trueman grimaced. 'Thanks,' he said, 'but I think I might leave it for the moment. I could do with some good strong coffee though.'

'Comin' right up,' Fiske said. 'There ain't a lot of room in here. I never could take to these places, anyway. I got a fire goin' outside. Why don't you join me?' Trueman nodded and made to go for the door when he was brought up sharp by a stab of pain.

'Here, let me help you,' Fiske said. Taking Trueman's arm, he placed it round his shoulder and together they staggered outside.

Almost immediately Trueman felt better. Maybe it was his imagination, but more likely it was the crisp clean air and sunshine that made the difference; Fiske's whiskey too. By the time he had a couple of tin mugs of thick black coffee inside him, he felt quite renewed.

'It was lucky for me you came by when you did,' he said. 'I figure I owe you my life. Those thugs weren't about to stop dishin' out the treatment any time soon.'

'It was my fault you got into that situation in the first place. I should have known better.'

'How do you mean? You couldn't be held responsible.'

'No, but it was because of me you were headin' for the Two Bar Cross in the first place.' Trueman winced as he leaned forward to pour more coffee.

'Here, I can do that for you.'

'Nope. I can manage. Tell me, who were those varmints?'

Fiske paused to gather his thoughts, pulling out a sack of Bull Durham and building himself a smoke as he did so. He passed the tobacco to Trueman who did likewise.

'They ride for an outfit called the Buckle M,' he said. 'It's the biggest spread around and it's run by a man called Cush Vogler. He's been tryin' to get his hands on the Two Bar Cross but so far he hasn't succeeded.'

'Because of you?'

'I ain't sayin' that. But he's been applying more and more pressure and I'm not sure how much longer the Two Bar can hang on.'

'What sort of pressure?'

'You've got experience of the treatment his boys like to give out. Those polecats who attacked you are some of Vogler's men. I know one of 'em. He's a gunslingin' varmint by name of Strangholt. I don't know about the others, but they're fairly typical.'

Trueman didn't reply but instead drew smoke into his lungs, appreciating the tobacco hit. He was really interested now.

'What else can you tell me about Vogler? Sounds like he employs some mighty ornery coyotes.'

'I don't know a lot about him. He's fairly new to the area, but since he arrived things have turned real bad. He's taken over a number of ranches and he more or less owns the township of Buzzard Roost.'

'It's aptly named. Owns the town or owns the people?'

'Both, I guess.'

Trueman paused to take a drag and mull over Fiske's words. Then he turned to the foreman.

'Were you genuine about that job?' he said.

'Sure. I'm short of men. Too many good folks have up and left since Vogler appeared on the scene.'

Trueman took another moment to finish his

coffee. 'I'd like to take on the job,' he said.

'After what happened? After what I just told you?'

'In the first place,' Trueman replied, 'I ain't about to let whoever did this to me get away with it. In the second place, I don't like bullies. And in the third place, I've come a considerable way to meet up with our friend Vogler.'

Fiske was the interested party now. He leaned forward, observing Trueman over the flames of the fire, his tin mug cupped in his hand. Trueman saw that the time had come to explain his presence in Buzzard Roost, and he proceeded to tell Fiske his story since the time he had come across Doc Drummond's wounded body.

'So you weren't exactly passin' through, then,' Fiske commented when Trueman had finished. 'What you say doesn't surprise me. There were rumours about Vogler's doin's but I never figured he operated over such a wide area. Stealin', cattle rustlin'. Yeah, that kinda fits.'

'Don't forget what happened to Drummond. I figure we're maybe just scratchin' the surface.'

There was a pause while each man thought about what the other had said. It was eventually broken by Fiske.

'So what are you figurin' to do?' he said.

'Like I say, I'd like to take up your offer. That'll give me time to size up the situation.' Suddenly Trueman laughed and immediately doubled up with the pain it caused. 'Don't get me wrong,' he gasped. 'If there's a job to be done I'll do it. Willingly.'

Fiske laughed in turn. 'Hell, the way you are right now, you're hardly in a fit state to be offerin' to do any kinda work. But the job's yours. And when it comes to dealin' with Vogler and his gunnies, I'll be right there alongside.'

'It could get mighty rough,' Trueman replied, 'but I got a feelin' that Vogler is gonna regret tryin' to run you off the Two Bar.'

It was one of Vogler's idiosyncratic pleasures every now and then to take a tour of his demesne, usually by day but sometimes by night. On these occasions he was usually accompanied by a couple or more of his gunslicks. Although he knew he had nothing to fear, past experience had taught him to be careful and be prepared for any eventualities. He was, therefore, glad he had them along on this occasion when a small group of horsemen appeared, riding towards him. He drew his own gun from its scabbard but quickly replaced it when he recognized Bigger at the head of them.

'Put your guns away,' he told his henchmen.

He watched as the group approached. Among the others was Micklum and his curiosity was aroused. He had sent them away to find Kettle's killer and deal with him, so what were they doing back already? Was it because they had carried out their mission? He continued to wait expectantly as Bigger came up and drew his horse to a halt, acknowledging Vogler by touching his hat. Vogler remained unmoved.

'I didn't expect you back here so quick,' he said. 'I hope you've done what I told you to do.'

'In a manner of speakin' we have,' Bigger said. His words irritated Vogler and he threw the gunnie a glowering look.

'It's like this,' Bigger said. 'We found out who was responsible for what happened in Dry Bluff. It's a man called Trueman. We got on his trail and it's brought us right back here.'

'What do you mean, back here?'

'You won't believe this,' Bigger said, 'but we followed him all the way to Buzzard Roost. And that ain't all. The bartender there says he was offered a job at the Two Bar Cross.'

'The Two Bar?'

'Yes, by the foreman there, a fella named Fiske. You might remember him.'

'I know who Fiske is.'

Vogler thought for a moment. Fiske? Hadn't that name come up recently? And then he remembered his recent conversation with Strangholt. What was it he had said? That they had found someone on the Buckle M range and had been in the process of dealing with him when Fiske arrived to put a stop to it? Most likely the man had not been on Buckle M property at all and Strangholt had been doing the trespassing. It made no difference one way or the other, but it was certainly a coincidence that Fiske's name should come up twice in such quick succession. Could there be a connection?

Then another thought struck him. Whether there was a connection or not, it seemed that this *hombre* Trueman was now at the Two Bar Cross. That made dealing with him a simple matter. On the other hand, it raised the question of just what was he doing here? Vogler turned his attention back to Bigger.

'Who are these people?' he asked, nodding in the direction of Bigger's fellow riders.

'Some of Kettle's gang. They want Trueman too.'

Vogler was thinking hard but he needed time to get everything straight.

'OK,' he said. 'You boys ride on and make yourselves at home in the bunkhouse. Bigger, I want you and Strangholt to report to me later at sundown. I need to hear the full story. Get movin'.'

Bigger wheeled his horse and rode away, accompanied by the others. Vogler watched them dwindle into the distance before turning his horse in the other direction. Bigger's arrival had interrupted his tour of the Buckle M, but he didn't intend it to change his plans. He had a good ride ahead of him and the best part of it was that, even so, he was only seeing a part of all the land he now owned. He would carry on up to the higher country where the cattle and other livestock he had stolen were hidden away in the lonely coulees.

As he rode he was thinking, and not just about what Bigger and Strangholt had told him. Gradually, he came to see that everything was coming together. He had in any case just about decided to attack the Two Bar Cross and take it by force. Now he had even more incentive. In the process, he could remove both Fiske and this newcomer Trueman from the scene. The more he thought about it, the more he liked it. He just needed to finalize his plans, and that would take no time at all.

On the second day after his arrival at the line cabin Trueman felt ready to ride. Fiske had been engaged in rounding up some stray cattle on the perimeter of the Two Bar Cross, and the pair of them set off to complete the task. It was hard work, especially for Trueman in his condition, but he was determined to carry out his part. They spent most of the day on the job and, as afternoon moved towards evening, drove the cattle back towards the corrals where they were being gathered and held prior to the branding. When the beeves had been securely penned Fiske turned to Trueman.

'I'll take you down to the bunkhouse,' he said, 'and you can meet some of the boys.'

The bunkhouse proved to be very quiet.

Trueman was about to comment when he remembered Fiske's words about the difficulty of finding suitable ranch hands. It seemed that Vogler and his gunnies had made their impression. Trueman chose one of the bunks and set out his few belongings.

'Grub'll be ready soon,' Fiske said. Trueman nodded. During the course of the day he had been thinking and he was ready to make a suggestion.

'Later,' he said, 'how about you and I take a look over the Buckle M?'

'Wouldn't that be trespassin'?' Fiske said.

'Yeah. That's why I reckon we might need the cover of darkness.'

Fiske laughed. 'What are you expectin' to find?' he said.

'I don't know. Maybe nothin'. But I figure there's rustled cattle hidden away somewhere, for one thing. Given the sort of coyote Vogler is, who knows what else we might uncover?'

'Now it's interestin' you should say that. As a matter of fact, some of our own critters seem to have gone missin'. I ain't done anythin' about it so far, but I'd sure be interested in takin' a look too. I was thinkin' about doin' that the other night when I came across you.'

'We might need to keep a lookout for Strangholt. He and his two buddies could be on some kinda night patrol.'

'Yeah, and maybe others too,' Fiske replied. Just

then the door to the bunkhouse flew open and a stoutly built man came in.

'Howdy Croft,' Fiske said, with a warning glance at Trueman. 'Come and meet a new recruit.' He made the introductions and then turned to Trueman. 'If there's anythin' you need to know, just ask Croft. I'll see you later.'

Morrison, the bartender, awoke in the still small hours with a raging headache and a parched throat. He had patched up his wounded forehead, and realized how lucky he had been not to lose an eye. That he had been attacked angered him. He got up from his mattress and made to go for the stairs leading down to the bar, but checked himself and instead returned to his room and poured a glass of water from the jug resting on a stand by the side of his bed. He paced up and down the room, taking a sip from the glass every now and then as he did so. He came to a halt beside a worn mirror and looked at his reflection.

What had happened to him? What had he come to? It was bad enough that he had ended up in a backwater like Buzzard Roost, but that wasn't the worst of it. It seemed that, somewhere along the line, he had lost his pride, his self-respect. There was a time when he would have stood up to a bully like Bigger. He would never have run scared like he was doing now. His features stared back at him; loose, sagging, unshaven, with bleary eyes and drooping mouth. What had brought him to this? It hadn't happened quickly. It had been a long, slow, debilitating process. The years had passed like locusts, casting dust over all his hopes and ambitions.

He turned away and wandered on to the balcony. The cold air struck him like a shower of rain and, raising his eyes, he gazed over the roofs of the little town to the hills beyond. Was it too late? Was there still time for him to gather his strength and rally again? And what about all those people sleeping in their beds, not peacefully but racked with fear of Vogler? Was it too late for them? Could they be roused from their torpor to face up to him? He took in deep draughts of air and felt his resolve grow. Could he trust himself? Would he wilt if the crisis came? But wasn't *this* the time of crisis? Perhaps it wasn't too late to take that chance, to put himself to the test. He turned back and sat on the edge of his bed, his brain pounding like a steam hammer, till at length he had a sense of calmness descending. He looked around the room and then, standing up, poured water into a bowl and began to douse his face, waiting for daylight.

It was very late when Trueman and Fiske rode away from the Two Bar Cross. They would have preferred the sky to be overcast, but it was a clear night; a full moon was up and the sky was filled with stars. They could see a long way, but so could any of Vogler's gunnies who happened to be around. They rode at a canter, their horses' hoofs beating a muffled rhythm on the grass. Ahead of them the foothills of the Bear Wallow range were sharply etched against the velvet sky. They rode for some little time until they crossed a narrow stream and Fiske brought them to a halt.

'That stream is the boundary between Two Bar Cross range and Buckle M,' he said.

'Right,' Trueman acknowledged.

Fiske pointed off to his right. 'The Buckle M ranch house lies in that direction. What do you want to do? Take a look there?'

Trueman thought for a moment before shaking his head. 'Nope,' he replied. 'If there's anything to be discovered, it's more likely to be in the direction of those hills.'

'Yeah. That seems to make sense. Let's push on then.'

They touched their spurs to their horses' flanks. After a time they began to pick out the dim shapes of cattle, standing singly or in small groups of two or three.

'Vogler is behindhand with the ropin' and brandin',' Trueman said.

'That don't surprise me, considerin' the type of man he employs. I'd be surprised if any of 'em have experience of range ridin'.'

They carried on, their senses alert and their eyes peering into the darkness. It seemed to Trueman that they must have covered a considerable distance; dawn was already beginning to lighten the sky when the landscape changed, with outcroppings of rock and patches of stunted vegetation. The hills had come close and the horses were beginning to strain.

'Let's stop for a while,' Fiske said, 'give 'em a breather.' They pulled up beside some rocks, dismounted and loosened the cinches to give the horses' backs some air. They were about to sit down when Trueman suddenly pointed towards the nearest hillside.

'Look! What's that?'

Fiske strained his eyes. After a few moments he saw what Trueman had seen: some tiny points of light.

'Cigarettes,' he said. 'There's somebody down there enjoyin' a smoke.'

'I could do with one myself.'

'It's a pity the wind, what there is of it, is blowin' in the wrong direction. We might have picked somethin' up.'

They listened closely but could hear nothing. The lights continued to glow intermittently, like faint fireflies.

'There's certainly more than one of 'em,' Fiske remarked. He got to his feet and drew his field glasses from his saddle-bags. Clamping them to his eyes, he watched closely. Suddenly he summoned Trueman.

'Quick, take a look,' he said. 'Those varmints are standin' right out in the open, and unless I'm very much mistaken, the one in the middle with the frock-coat is Vogler himself.'

Trueman took the glasses. Three men were standing together; he concentrated his attention on Vogler.

'You can't miss him,' Fiske said. 'He always dresses like that.'

The men were apparently talking together. Finally they turned and quickly vanished from sight. Trueman handed the glasses back.

'So that's Vogler,' he said.

'Did you get a good sight of him?' Fiske asked.

'Good enough,' Trueman replied. They continued to watch until the lights disappeared. Trueman thought he heard the snicker of a horse but he couldn't be certain.

'Now what would Vogler be doin' out here, or anyone else for that matter, apart from us?' Trueman remarked.

'I don't know, but we'd best be careful what we're doin'.' Fiske looked towards the hills. 'I reckon we should take a little detour to avoid runnin' into them,' he said. 'There's an old Indian trail leads along by a waterfall. I ain't been there in a long time but I think I can find it.'

Trueman nodded. 'Let's do it,' he said.

Once they had assured themselves that the horses were rested, they climbed back into leather and continued riding. The hills loomed over them now, but as they began to climb they found that they were less steep than they had imagined. The horses sure-footedly picked their way upwards, the only sound being the faint creak of leather. The trail they were following was fairly straightforward and Fiske was looking for the cut-off which would lead near the waterfall in the direction in which they had seen the flickering lights. The trail led them round an outcrop of granite, beyond which there appeared to be traces of a trail leading off to their left.

'I don't know if this is what I had in mind,' Fiske said, 'but I reckon it's goin' in the right direction.'

'Are we still on Buckle M property?' Trueman queried.

'Yeah. Their range extends right up into the Bear Wallows.'

The new trail was steeper and the horses were beginning to find the going more difficult. When they reached what had appeared to be the crest they found it was only a ledge and the trail continued climbing. Rather abruptly, however, they rounded another outcrop and found themselves looking down at a narrow valley, sheltered on all sides by the surrounding hills. But what was really unexpected was the sight of grazing cattle.

'So those stories about Vogler were true,' Fiske said. 'I'll bet you a dollar to a dime that those critters are rustled stock.'

'There are probably more hidden valleys like this,' Trueman commented. 'Vogler could have an entire herd stashed away up here.'

They looked closely for any sign of the men they had seen but the place seemed deserted; then Fiske's keen eyes spotted something else interesting, hidden away at the far side of the valley.

'Now what the hell is that?' he murmured. He reached for his field glasses and took a lingering look. 'It's an old cabin,' he said, passing the glasses to Trueman.

'Not so old either, I reckon,' Trueman said as he peered through them. 'At least, it looks to me like it's been lived in. There's a pile of logs right up against the wall. And what's that structure standin' in the yard? What do you make of it?' He handed the glasses back for Fiske to take another peek.

'I'm not sure,' Fiske said, 'but I got a hunch it could be some kind of oil pump.' He put the glasses away and sat for a moment in thought. Then he suddenly snapped his fingers.

'By Jiminy, I think I've got it; I mean the reason Vogler is so keen to get his hands on the Two Bar Cross.' He turned to Trueman. 'I've been with Two Bar a long while and I reckon I know it pretty well. In certain places there are oil seeps. I never thought much of it because it never struck me as bein' significant. But I gather that oil is goin' to be mighty important in the future. If I'm right, that would explain why Vogler decided to set himself up here in the first place.'

'I'll take your word for it,' Trueman replied. 'This talk of oil doesn't mean anythin' to me.'

'I'm willin' to bet I'm right. They've been pumpin' oil in Pennsylvania for a few years now. At a place called Titusville. Hell, maybe Vogler even had a hand in that.'

'You want to take a closer look?' Trueman asked.

By way of answer Fiske pointed away from the cabin. Trueman glanced in that direction and after a few moments saw a couple of riders.

'Looks like our friends are comin' back,' Fiske said. 'In any case, I figure I've seen enough and we've taken too long already.' He raised himself in the stirrups and took a good look around. 'It's already gettin' light. Retracin' our steps will be dangerous.'

'It's a risk we'll just have to take.'

'I got a better idea. I figure if we circle the valley part of the way and take another trail we should come out near the waterfall. There's a quicker way down from that point, leadin' to the Two Bar Cross.'

'I thought you hadn't been up here in a long time.'

'I never forget an old trail,' Fiske replied. 'You never know when the knowledge might be useful.'

With a last look across the valley he turned his horse's head and led the way along a narrow track, taking care to keep himself just below the skyline.

When they had travelled about halfway round the rim, he turned his horse away and began to descend the hill before taking another line that led them higher again. As they rode, Trueman's ears picked up faint sounds, which steadily increased in volume.

'What's that?' he asked.

'The waterfall. It doesn't amount to much.'

They rounded a bend and the fall was finally revealed, the water dropping for a distance of about fifty feet before continuing to flow in a narrow stream down the hillside. The sky presaged dawn and in the gathering light Trueman could distinguish the shadowy outlines of buildings on the plain below.

'Buzzard Roost,' Fiske said.

They looked down on the little town as it slept, dark and silent under the whirling stars, before Fiske eventually touched his spurs to his horse's flanks and they continued to ride. The town was soon lost to view as they descended a twisting trail that brought them down more and more gradually, till eventually they were back on level ground.

'We're not safe yet,' Fiske remarked. 'There's some dispute, but most of the land around here still belongs to the Buckle M. We ain't likely to run across anyone, though.'

They carried on riding as the first rays of daylight began to spread across the sky. Trueman was unsure of just exactly where they were and it came as a surprise to him when eventually they rode under a sign suspended from a wooden beam which bore the inscription: 2 ¬ +

'I guess we're home,' Fiske said.

They carried on riding as dawn's rays spread across the sky from the eastern horizon. The lowing of cattle still waiting to be rounded up sounded on the air and from somewhere a cock crowed as they caught their first glimpse of the ranch house.

Despite his hard-headed business acumen and his ruthlessness in terms of getting what he wanted, Vogler had a solid streak of superstition in his make-up. The more he thought about Trueman, the more uncomfortable he felt. When he got back to the ranch house after his night in the hills, the question raised itself more insistently. Who was Trueman? Why had he arrived on the scene at Buzzard Roost? He almost seemed like a kind of nemesis. So far he had accounted for Kettle and Swain with surprisingly little difficulty. He seemed to lead a charmed life, which made it all the more frustrating that he had escaped Strangholt when that gunslinging yahoo had him in his power. If Fiske hadn't come by and intervened. . . .

He comforted himself with the thought that Trueman's number was up. He had made a mistake by joining the Two Bar Cross. The Two Bar wouldn't be able to put up any opposition once he,

Vogler, went up against it. Trueman and Fiske couldn't escape; they would be gunned down along with anyone else who dared to oppose him and the Two Bar would be his. Still, he had a nagging feeling that he couldn't quite shake off. Lifting a bell which stood on his desk, he rang it and presently one of his lackeys appeared.

'Yes, Mr Vogler?'

'Get hold of Bigger and Strangholt and tell them to get over here pronto,' Vogler said. The man left and after a little time there was a knock on the door.

'Come in!' Vogler called. The door opened and the two gunslingers appeared.

'Do you two do anythin' to earn your pay?' Vogler snapped.

'We were just about to do some work at the stables.'

'If so, you can forget it,' Vogler said. 'I've got a real job for the two of you which should be more to your likin'.'

'Yeah, boss. What's that?'

'We're just about ready to hit the Two Bar Cross. Before we do that, however, I'd like to deal with this *hombre* Trueman.'

'You said we ride the day after tomorrow. Couldn't it wait till then?'

'It could, but after what happened down in Dry Bluff I kinda got a hankerin' to deal with Trueman personally.'

Strangholt grinned, revealing his broken, tobacco-stained teeth.

'I'd sure like to get Trueman in my hands again,' he muttered.

'Yes, and I've no doubt the same applies to Bigger. That's why I want you to head on over to the Two Bar and find him. Bring him back here alive if you can, but dead or alive, I want him.'

'It'll be a pleasure,' Bigger said.

'Just in case you have any problems recognizing the varmint, by the way, make sure you take Krall along with you,' Vogler added. 'It shouldn't take you too long. Trueman's's got to be cuttin' cattle someplace. If anyone else gets in the way, shoot 'em.'

'Sure thing. We'll be back with Trueman's head on a plate before you know it.'

'Preferably still on his body,' Vogler replied. 'Leave me to do the rest.' Bigger and Strangholt both broke into ugly laughter.

'OK,' Vogler said. 'What are you waitin' for? You got two days before we ride. That should be plenty.'

He watched as the two gunslicks turned and went out of the door. When it had shut behind them he got to his feet, walked to a cabinet, and poured himself a stiff drink. He sat down at his desk and took a sip. Ah, that was good! He was feeling a lot better. This was just the sort of job Bigger and Strangholt relished. Maybe he was just a little under the weather. He had really nothing to fear from Trueman, and if it fell to his lot to deliver the final, knock-out blow, so much the better.

CHAPTER SIX

It was late in the afternoon when Fiske returned to the ranch house, having been working with Trueman on the repair of some fences. As he rode into the yard and dismounted, the door of the bunkhouse opened and Croft came out.

'You got a visitor,' he said.

'Oh yeah? And who might that be?'

'Dan Morrison.'

'Morrison? You mean the bartender at the Black Diamond saloon in Buzzard Roost?'

Croft nodded. 'I said he could wait in the bunkhouse, but he decided to take a walk. He should be back soon.'

'Now I wonder what he could want?' Fiske replied. 'Thanks, Croft.'

He tied his horse to the hitch rack and made his way into the ranch house. There was some paperwork he had been neglecting for a long time and he needed to get on with it. He sat down at a small roll-top desk and got out the papers. After a time he pushed them aside. It was no good pretending otherwise: paperwork wasn't his forte. It was at times like this he wished Crosby was there, but the owner had been called back East on family business and it was uncertain when he would be back. He was about to nerve himself for the task again when there was a knock on the door. He got to his feet, walked across the room and opened it. Morrison was standing outside.

'Howdy,' said Fiske. 'Come on in.'

The bartender followed Fiske into the room. 'It's a long time since I was last here,' he remarked. 'I was just takin' a walk while I waited. It's a nice place.'

'Take a seat. I reckon you could probably use a drink,' Fiske said. He went to a small cabinet and produced a bottle of whiskey and a couple of tumblers.

'Makes a change for someone else to be doin' the honours,' Morrison remarked.

As Morrison took a sip of the whiskey Fiske observed him. He knew the bartender from his trips to town, but it seemed there was something different about him. He had tidied himself up, had a shave. His shirt and trousers looked new and Fiske was surprised to see he was wearing a gunbelt and holster, from which protruded the ivory handle of a six-gun. At the same time, he was sitting awkwardly and seemed to be somewhat ill at ease. Fiske was curious to know his business, but he waited for the bartender to explain. Morrison took another swig of the whiskey, then faced Fiske.

'I guess you're wonderin' what I'm doin' here?' he said. Fiske nodded. 'The truth is, I've got somethin' of a confession to make. Do you know a man called Bigger?'

Fiske was startled but didn't show it. 'Yes,' he said, 'I know him and I don't like him. He's one of Vogler's gun-totin' hardcases.'

'Yeah, that's him. Well, he was in the Black Diamond the other night, him and some of his cronies, causin' trouble.' Morrison paused, as if finding it difficult to continue. 'The long and short of it is,' he resumed, 'that they got me to tell them about you and that feller Trueman.'

'What do you mean? Tell them what?'

'That you'd offered Trueman a job and he'd gone off to the Two Bar Cross. I didn't think. It was only later that I figured I might have said too much.'

'Why would you think that?'

'Bigger is unstable. There's no knowin' what he might do. I don't know. I just got to thinkin' I'd maybe given somethin' away you wouldn't want Bigger to know.' He paused for a moment before continuing:

'That's not all. There was somethin' else Bigger said, somethin' about the Two Bar Cross gettin' what was comin' to it. I think that was it. It probably doesn't mean anything. Bigger was in a rage. He didn't know what he was sayin'.' Fiske drank the remaining whiskey in his tumbler.

'I appreciate you tellin' me this,' Fiske said.

'I thought you ought to know.'

'You did right. And don't worry. You've nothin' to blame yourself for.'

'Yes, I do. For too long I've put up with Bigger and others like him. Because they ride for Vogler, they figure they can do what they like. Well, I think it's about time I stood up to him. And not just me: the rest of the townsfolk too. Because I work in the Black Diamond, I guess I get to deal with more of Vogler's hardcases than most, but we're all in the same boat. I've spoken to some of the men and there are a few others like me willin' to take a stand. Maybe not willin'. That would be puttin' too fine a point on it. But prepared to stand up to Vogler if they have to.'

'Is that why you're carryin' those sidearms?'

Morrison grinned sheepishly. 'I knew how to use them once. I figure I can do it again.'

Fiske was thinking hard. What Morrison had said about Bigger's threatening the Two Bar Cross came as no real surprise. It only confirmed what he suspected. Vogler had been applying pressure for Fiske to sell. It was only a matter of time till he took it one step further. That time seemed to have come.

'Do you mean what you say?' he asked.

'About what?'

'About bein' prepared to stand up to Vogler if it came to it.'

'Yes, of course. I ain't meant anythin' so serious in a long time.'

Fiske gave him an intent look. There was a steely set to the man's features and Fiske felt that he was genuine.

'It might soon come to that,' he said. 'I think there's a real confrontation brewin' between Vogler and the Two Bar Cross.'

'If there is, I'd like to be there,' Morrison replied. Fiske spent a few moments in thought before saying more to the bartender.

'Listen,' he said. 'Get on back to Buzzard Roost and round up any of the townsfolk who are prepared to fight Vogler. Then get back here with them as quick as you can. If there's goin' to be a showdown it's goin' to be right here and the fate of the town is goin' to be in the balance just as much as the Two Bar Cross. If Vogler gets his way here, life won't be worth livin' for the townsfolk. Vogler will be in total charge. He and his gunnies will do just as they like and there won't be anybody to even attempt to stop him. You hear what I'm sayin'?'

'Yes, I do, and I think you're right.' Morrison got to his feet. 'I'll leave right now and get back to town as quick as possible. With any luck, I'll be able to round up a few willin' fighters.' He made for the door, then stopped on its threshold.

'Thanks, Fiske,' he said.

'Thanks for what?'

'For givin' me back my self-respect. For givin' me a chance to make good. I won't let you down.' He turned and went through the door.

Fiske moved to the window and watched him as he made his way to the stables to get his horse. His back was straight and there was a purposive set to his stride. Even if he was unable to persuade any of his fellow townsmen to take up arms, Fiske felt sure that he had one man at least on whom he could rely.

Bigger and Strangholt, accompanied by the weasel-like Krall, made no bones about the issue of riding over rangeland that belonged to the Two Bar Cross. Trespassing wasn't one of their concerns. It was well known that the place was undermanned and if they did meet with anyone, they knew how to deal with him. It didn't worry them, either, that they had no better plan when they got there than to keep their eyes open. As they neared the Two Bar Cross it was Krall who drew their attention to the deficiencies of the scheme.

'I've been thinkin',' he said.

'You don't get paid to do that,' Bigger replied. Something about Krall irritated him.

'What have you been thinkin'?' Strangholt said.

'Well, it's like this. I haven't got anythin' against

lookin' for Trueman, but what happens if he's not alone? What happens if he's with somebody else?'

'You wouldn't be gettin' cold feet?' Bigger said. 'After all, you didn't do a very good job last time you tried dealin' with Trueman.' Krall ignored the comment. He was helped out by Strangholt.

'Maybe you got a point. So what are you suggestin'?'

'Wherever he is, at some stage Trueman has to get back to the ranch house.'

'When he's finished workin', you mean?'

'Yes. He'll head for the bunkhouse just like anyone else. We've worked at ranchin' before. We know the routines. So why don't we just wait for him somewhere along the trail? We'd be pretty sure to catch him that way. Remember, Mr Vogler said he'd prefer to have Trueman alive.'

Krall had grave doubts that either Bigger or Strangholt in reality knew much about the routines of ranching, but then his own experience was strictly limited. However, he had made his point and Strangholt at least seemed to consider it.

'Do either of you know the Two Bar Cross?' Krall queried.

'Some,' Strangholt replied. 'If you're askin' about the lie of the land, I could think of places that might suit.'

'With sufficient cover?'

'Yeah, I reckon so.'

Bigger spat on the ground. 'We're wastin' time,'

he said. 'Let's get goin'.'

'Maybe Krall's got a point,' Strangholt said. 'We could check it out at least. We might as well ride one way as another.'

Bigger gave Krall a withering stare. 'Are you sure you'd even recognize Trueman?' he said. 'Seems to me like maybe you were makin' yourself scarce last time.'

This time Krall was stung but he was sensible enough not to show it. He knew he was no match for Bigger, and he hadn't survived as long as he had without being canny.

'I'd recognize him,' he said. 'Isn't that why you've got me along?'

'There ain't any question of us not recognizin' him. I'd know the varmint a mile off,' Strangholt rapped.

They sat their horses in silence for a few moments, each one of them angry in his own way. Then, still without speaking but as if by mutual consent, they rowlled their horses and moved on again.

Following what Morrison had said about the threat to the Two Bar Cross, which only confirmed his own conclusions, Fiske called a meeting of his ranch hands.

'In view of what I've just said,' he concluded, 'I'd understand if anyone wanted to take the opportunity to leave before things get hot. You all signed up as ranch hands. None of you signed to a fight.' He stopped and waited. There was a hush followed by a few whispered colloquies among the men. Then Croft stood up.

'Nobody's plannin' to leave,' he said. 'Whichever way you put it, we all signed to the brand.'

'Are you sure about it?' Fiske said. 'There'd be no hard feelin's and I guarantee now that once this has blown over, anyone who wanted it would have his job back.'

'Like I said, nobody's plannin' to leave.'

'We're all stayin',' a voice called. 'We ain't about to buckle in to Vogler or anybody else!'

'Thanks. I sure appreciate it,' Fiske said. He paused, clearly moved by the show of loyalty, but quickly resumed his theme.

'Now that's all been decided,' he said, 'it seems to me like we ought to be decidin' how best to go about defendin' the Two Bar.' There was another murmur as people began to voice their opinions, then Trueman stepped forward.

'I'm new to the Two Bar,' he said, 'and maybe I'm speakin' out of turn. Whatever you boys decide, I'll go along with, but it seems to me that it's important to take the initiative.'

'How do you mean?' Fiske asked.

'We could sit right here and try to defend the ranch house. I can see reasons why that might have advantages, but I reckon they're outweighed by the disadvantages. In particular, I don't like the idea of us gettin' tied down. Vogler could just sit back and starve us out or burn us out. No, I figure we ought to go out and meet him and hope to catch him by surprise before he ever gets this far.' His comments were greeted by a babble of voices before Fiske spoke again.

'I reckon Trueman is right,' he said. 'I've been thinkin' the same, and it's my opinion that the best place to catch Vogler and his boys would be as they cross the stream at Fletcher's Ford.'

'What if they don't come that way?' someone shouted.

'It's a chance, but only a slim one. The main trail from the Buckle M comes that way. They wouldn't have any reason to take any of the back trails. Even if they did, we wouldn't be any the worse off.'

'It would help if the stream was swollen,' Croft commented, 'but that isn't likely.'

'Maybe not, but they'll still be concentratin' on gettin' across. There are banks on either side. OK, they're not steep, but they're steep enough to slow 'em down and there's cover along the stream bottom and on the slopes overlookin' it. Throw in the element of surprise Trueman was just mentionin', and we might have a chance.'

The discussion broke out again and heads began to nod. Croft, acting as the men's spokesman, got back to his feet.

'The feelin' seems to be that it's as good a plan as any. Unless anyone's got a better one, I think we should go ahead with it.'

Fiske looked about for confirmation from the others, and when it was clear that everyone was in agreement he brought the more formal part of the meeting to a close so that they could begin to discuss the plan in more detail.

Trueman drew his horse to a halt to observe a lone cow. It held its head sideways and kept shaking it. With his practised eye, he knew the cause of its odd behaviour: screw worm. Riding closer, he dropped from the saddle, drew a bottle of screw-worm medicine from his saddle-bags, and approached the animal, trying to ignore the peculiar odour it emitted. The medicine contained mainly carbolic acid and axle grease and he swabbed the animal's wounds with it.

'Damn blowflies!' he muttered.

The words were hardly out of his mouth before the boom of a rifle sounded from close by. His horse reared and then took off, but Trueman had the presence of mind to seize hold of the reins before it had gathered speed, and swing himself on board. Second and third shots rang out and he thought he saw a flash among some rocks. He bent low over the horse's mane as it thundered along till he felt he was beyond range of his assailant's gun. He sat up and continued to let the horse have its head till eventually he slowed it down and brought it to a halt. Who had fired the shots? There could be no doubt that they were aimed at him and he had only good luck to thank that he hadn't been hit.

He turned his horse round and began to ride back, but he knew there was small chance of catching his attacker. Once the man realized he had failed in his attempt to kill Trueman, he would waste no time in getting away. Trueman was taken by surprise when he saw a rider in the distance, who seemed to be coming towards him. He reached for his scabbard and withdrew his Sharps rifle. The approaching figure was still some distance away and Trueman pulled up in order to take a look through his field glasses. There was something familiar about the rider. He was not carrying any weapon and was riding quite openly. He took a closer look, convinced that it couldn't be the person who had been doing the shooting, then he recognized him. It was the bartender from the Black Diamond saloon in Buzzard Roost. Trueman put the glasses back and spurred his horse forwards. As they came close the man raised his arm in greeting.

'You were taking a chance,' Trueman said. The barman looked puzzled. 'Didn't you hear those shots?' Trueman asked.

'I thought I heard somethin'. Why, what happened?'

Trueman quickly explained the situation. When he had finished Morrison's expression became quite animated.

'If someone was taking a shot at you,' he said, 'I reckon I know who it was.'

'Yeah? Who?'

'A man called Bigger. He was askin' questions about you at the saloon. And it looks like he's got a couple of other men ridin' with him.'

'How do you know that?'

'I've just seen them. They were ridin' hard in that direction.' He pointed over his shoulder.

'I don't know anyone by name of Bigger.'

'He's one of Vogler's hired men.'

'Maybe you'd better explain what you mean and what you're doin' here. Fiske said somethin' about you comin' over.'

Quickly, Morrison outlined his own story, finishing with his arrival at the Two Bar Cross and his talk with Fiske.

'I'm just ridin' back from town. I can tell you, things are stirrin' back there. There are half a dozen men willin' to take a stand against Vogler if they're called on to do it.'

Trueman listened with interest, but his thoughts were largely elsewhere. If what Morrison said was right, the men who had attacked him were not far away and he knew in which direction to find them. It was slightly odd that they seemed to be heading in the direction of the Two Bar Cross rather than away from it, but there could easily be a reason. What was the most likely? Suddenly he had a flash of inspiration. One reason could be that they were heading that way in order to lay a trap for him. They had probably come on him by chance and one of them at least had not been able to resist taking a pot. He turned to Morrison.

'Are you in earnest when you say you want to take a stand against Vogler?'

'Yes, of course.'

'Then you can start doin' it right now, if you're sure that man you saw riding away was this *hombre* Bigger.'

'I'm pretty sure. And I'm also pretty sure that one of the other two was a gunslinger by name of Strangholt.'

'Strangholt! That clinches it.' Trueman recalled the night he had taken a beating. The leader of that little gang had been named Strangholt. He felt a surge of energy. Maybe he would have his opportunity for payback quicker than he had thought.

'Listen,' he said, 'I'm gonna try and catch up with those three. If you like, you can ride along with me, or else you can carry on to the Two Bar.'

There was a grin on the barman's face. 'Try and stop me from ridin' with you,' he said.

'Good. But be careful and do exactly what I tell you to do: especially if it comes to a fight.'

'Whatever you say,' Morrison replied. 'I'm ready.'

They turned their horses and began to ride. Morrison knew the direction the gunslicks had taken and pretty soon they came upon their sign. It wasn't difficult to follow. Even if Morrison hadn't told him, Trueman would have been able to work out that there were three riders. Every so often he drew them to a halt and took a look ahead through his field glasses. He didn't want to take the chance of being ambushed again.

Pretty soon they were following a trail that would lead them back to the ranch house and Trueman knew that if he was correct in his surmise, Bigger and his companions would be looking out for a place to hide themselves. Had they seen Morrison? Trueman thought not, and even if they had, he would have been nothing more to them than a lone ranch hand. All the same, it paid to be cautious.

He drew out his glasses again and examined the terrain. Up ahead the trail ran down through some rocks and boulders. They couldn't be too far from the ranch house. He handed the glasses to Morrison.

'What do you think?' he said.

'I can't see anythin'.'

'Nope. They wouldn't be that careless. But that's just the sort of spot they'd be lookin' for.'

Morrison handed the glasses back. 'So, what do we do now?'

'We take a little detour,' Trueman replied.

'If they're there, they might be able to see us.'

'I doubt it,' Trueman said, 'and besides, even if they can, from that range they won't know who we are. We could be just another couple of ranch hands.'

He took a long look about him. 'OK. At this point we split up. I go off to the left; you go off to the right. I want to get among those rocks and catch 'em unawares. You get up as close as you can without being seen but stay at a little distance. When you hear shootin', then come on in. But be careful. Make sure you aren't seen. You might need to cover the final part on foot.'

Morrison nodded. 'You take care too,' he said.

'Right. Let's go!'

Trueman wheeled his horse and soon began to gallop. He glanced round, to see that Morrison was already a fair distance away. He had a moment of doubt. Would Morrison prove reliable? He might be the opposite and give the game away. Maybe he should have dealt with Bigger by himself and sent Morrison on to the ranch house. Well, it was too late to do anything about it now. There was no chance but to carry on with the plan.

He continued riding, bending his path in a broad semicircle so as to come at the gunslicks from the appropriate angle. He was careful to keep himself concealed as far as possible, but when he calculated he was at the right distance from the rocks he brought the Steel Dust to a halt and slid from the saddle. He threw the reins over the horse's head and then, taking his rifle, began to pick his way forward on foot, keeping to whatever cover presented itself.

Before long he crested a slight rise of land and saw the rocks ahead of him. To his right he could see an extension of the trail he and Morrison had been riding. The gunnies, if they were concealed among the rocks, would be facing that way, looking out for him to come along it. He looked hard but could see no signs of movement. For a moment he regretted having left his field glasses behind, but he hadn't wanted to be encumbered with them. Selecting a route that offered the best prospects for concealment, he began to creep forward again.

He moved slowly, keeping low and being careful to make no sound. He listened closely for any noise from the direction of the rocks, but the wind was blowing from the wrong quarter. He was looking out for horses but they were well hidden. Then, just as he was wondering whether he might have been wrong and the whole enterprise would turn out to be a wild-goose chase, he heard a faint whinny. It was his first indication that the gunslicks might be hidden among the rocks after all.

He crept on, cradling his rifle, till he reached the rocky outcrop, where he crouched behind the nearest boulder. He waited, looking and listening; awake to any indication of the gunmen's presence. When nothing was forthcoming he determined to press on. His attention was divided now between observing where he placed his feet and being alert to what was around him. For all he knew, the gunslicks could be around any corner, hiding behind the next rock.

He came to a large slab of rock and as he rounded it he was taken aback by the sudden sight of the horses. Apart from the one whinny, he had heard nothing. They were standing at a little distance, concealed partly by anther rocky outcrop and a screening patch of bushes. He pulled up short. Had the gunslicks left them close by where they were waiting or at a distance?

He had a sudden idea and creeping forward, approached them with the utmost caution. They began to shift at his approach but, whispering quietly, he reached out and began to untie them. His plan was turn them loose and then take up a position in the bushes to be ready for the gunslicks when they realized what had happened. Just as he was unfastening the last rope he heard a shout:

'Drop the rifle!'

Involuntarily, he turned to see who had uttered it. Standing next to the big rock he had just come round was the figure of a man with a rifle trained on him. At the same moment the bushes parted and two other men emerged, their rifles similarly levelled. Without thinking, he dropped down behind the horses, shouting loudly as he did so to scare them, and striking the nearest one with the butt of his rifle across its rump. The animal reared, spreading panic among the other two. For a moment there was pandemonium as the horses broke loose, tossing their heads and twisting and turning this way and that before starting to gallop pell-mell in different directions. The confusion was enough to give Trueman time to roll away into the partial cover of the bushes.

He wasn't an instant too soon as a hail of bullets crashed into the undergrowth and ricocheted loudly from the rocks. The two gunslicks who had emerged from the bushes were so close that his ears were temporarily deafened and the flashes of flame seemed close enough to singe him. That was his salvation. The gunnies were too close to take proper aim and their bullets flew over his head, ripping through the foliage like hail. Getting to his knees, Trueman swung his rifle up and round and began pumping lead. He heard a scream and a curse and then the thudding of boots.

He sprang forward, bent low, in time to see two of the gunnies disappear round the rock. The third lay on the ground, but Trueman couldn't tell whether he was dead or alive and he wasn't foolish enough to expose himself to the mercy of the gunnies' rifles to find out. Instead he darted to his left and began to climb the rocks in an effort to gain an advantage over the two remaining gunslicks.

A rifle cracked and shards of stone flew high and wide as a bullet smashed into the rock just above him. The shot came from overhead and Trueman instinctively turned and swung his rifle upwards, opening fire as he did so. One of the gunslicks was standing partly exposed on a rock. Trueman hadn't taken proper aim and as the reverberations of his shot rang out, mingling with the report of the gunman's rifle as he fired again, he thought he had missed. The gunslick's bullet tore through the shoulder of his jacket and he felt a hot surge of pain as the bullet grazed his flesh. The shock made him drop his rifle. He fell sideways, anticipating another slug, but instead the man above him continued to stand immobile.

In those moments of strange inertia Trueman recognized the ugly features of Strangholt, the man who had beaten him. Suddenly Strangholt swayed and then collapsed like a felled tree, bouncing off the rocks as he landed head first on the hard ground below. Trueman had no time to think about him because immediately afterwards he heard the sound of boots scraping on rock; he realized that the third man was trying to make his getaway.

Trueman struggled to his feet. Ignoring his fallen rifle and clutching his shoulder, he set off in hot pursuit. His injury, rather than slowing him down, seemed to provide a spur, and he climbed and scrambled his way with a new influx of energy.

He wasn't sure which way the man had gone, but he just kept plunging on till he had a sudden glimpse of him a little way ahead.

The man was running like someone possessed, but Trueman was gaining on him. He seemed to become aware of Trueman's presence and turned to fire. A couple of bullets went singing past Trueman's ear but he kept on, ignoring them. The man was out in the open now and suddenly he pulled up, his gun in his hand. So hectic had Trueman's pursuit been that he had not thought to draw his own weapon. Panting and heaving with the effort of running, he came to a halt in front of the man he had been pursuing.

'I take it you're Trueman,' the man hissed.

Trueman drew in deeps draughts of air in an effort to gain control of himself. Even as he did so, he realized that the man confronting him must be similarly affected.

'And I guess you must be Bigger,' he managed to reply.

'You've put some people to a lot of trouble, Trueman,' the man breathed.

'A lot of low-down polecats,' Trueman replied. His words seemed to anger Bigger and the man's contorted features twisted even further.

'You and that varmint Fiske are gonna pay. It's almost a pity that you ain't gonna be around when Fiske gets what's due to him tomorrow. Right now, you'd do better to start beggin' for mercy,' he replied. 'Now, throw away your gunbelt and get down on your knees.'

Trueman hesitated for just a moment before complying with the first part of the instructions. When he had done so, he allowed his eyes to flicker and fix on something beyond his assailant.

'I think it's maybe you should be gettin' down on your knees,' he said.

'Do it! Now!'

'Look behind you, Bigger.'

'You don't expect me to fall for that one.'

Before Trueman could do or say anything, there was a loud explosion from behind Bigger and a bullet went singing through the air. Bigger turned.

'Krall' he exclaimed. 'What the hell. . . ?'

Almost before the words were out of his mouth another shot rang out. Again the bullet seemed to miss its target but this time Bigger's reaction was instantaneous as his six-gun barked and Krall fell heavily to the ground. Bigger quickly spun round and fired at Trueman, but where Trueman had been standing was just empty air. He felt Trueman's hand grasp his ankles and he went over in a tangle. As he brought up his gun, Trueman's boot caught him in the chest and the shot he fired flew harmlessly into the air.

In a matter of moments he had recovered but that was enough time for Trueman to have retrieved one of his six-guns. Bigger still had the edge and his finger had already closed on the trigger as Trueman got off a shot. The two explosions sounded almost simultaneously but when the smoke cleared it was Trueman who remained standing, while Bigger had hit the ground. Trueman waited for some reaction from the gunslick before stepping forward. One glance was enough to show him that he had nothing more to fear from Bigger. Trueman's one shot had caught him square between the eyes and he was dead. Trueman moved away to where Krall was lying in a pool of blood; he recognized the lifeless corpse as the man he had first shot in the bushes. Somehow, despite being wounded, he had managed to get back into the action.

The only thing that puzzled Trueman was why Krall had opted to go for Bigger rather than him. Maybe the man's condition had caused him to be confused. Maybe he had some grudge against Bigger and had decided to deal with him first. After all, at the time of his reappearance Trueman had been unarmed. What the hell, he thought, they're all out of it now.

As he was preparing to move away he heard a sound behind him. He spun round, ready to shoot, when he recognized the features of Morrison.

'Hell,' he snapped, 'that's the second time you almost got shot.'

'Are you OK, Trueman? I got here as quick as I could when I heard the shootin'.'

Trueman let out a huge sigh of relief and exhaustion.

'You're a bit later than I would have liked,' he said, 'but at least you're here.'

CHAPTER SEVEN

Vogler's men were saddled up and ready to go, but there was no sign of Vogler himself. He had been in a very bad mood the previous day and, while a number of reasons had been put forward, nobody knew for sure why. The opposite should have been true. The time of waiting was over. They were ready to go and pretty soon the Two Bar Cross would be his.

For Vogler himself, however, that prospect was overshadowed by the failure of Bigger, Strangholt and Krall to return to the Buckle M. Why were they taking so long? What could have happened to them? He couldn't work it out. Surely, it was an easy enough mission he had entrusted to them? He had been expecting them to bring in Trueman, dead or alive. But it hadn't happened. Whoever he was and whatever he was up to, Trueman seemed to thwart him at every turn, and it reawakened the superstitious feelings he had been having concerning Trueman.

The previous night he had been drinking heavily, and he had even thought of staying behind and letting his men deal with the Two Bar without him. With the coming of morning his mood had improved and he had begun to feel more positive. Whatever had become of his three gunslicks, it didn't matter. He had plenty of men at his disposal and this time he would make sure that Trueman didn't escape his vengeance or the wrath that was about to be visited on the Two Bar Cross. He didn't intend getting involved in any real fighting himself, but he strapped on his guns with a resolute air.

As he stepped on to the veranda of the Buckle M, his men greeted him with a shout and a cheer and a couple of the wilder elements began firing into the air. He held up his hand as a sign for them to desist, then addressed them in a booming tone.

'This is it, men! This the moment we've been waitin' for, and I can assure each and every one of you that you'll be well rewarded. You know what's to be done, so let's do it! Let's go and have fun!'

The uproar broke out again as Vogler stepped down from the veranda and mounted his horse, his men following his example. Vogler was beginning to enjoy the role and he felt like a conqueror as he raised his arm as the signal to move and yelled out one last time:

'Let's go get 'em!'

Fiske had been up and about far earlier than Vogler, and before the time Vogler rode away from the Buckle M his men had taken their allotted places along the banks of the stream Vogler had to cross. Some were concealed in bushes and trees overlooking the stream and others were in place higher up along the banks. As the sun began to climb in the sky he and Trueman sat their horses and surveyed the scene.

'What do you think, Trueman?' Fiske asked. 'I ain't much of a fightin' man. Is there anythin' else we could do?'

'I don't reckon so. The only thing we've got to worry about is whether we've chosen the right spot for a fight. There must be other places Vogler could choose to cross the stream, or even get to the Two Bar some other way.'

'There's no way of knowin' for certain, but this is the fordin' place.'

Trueman looked down on the water. 'It ain't exactly a swirlin' torrent,' he replied.

'Maybe I should have left somebody back at the ranch to give us warnin' in case Vogler does come some other way.'

'We can't afford to spare anybody,' Trueman said.

Fiske took another sweeping look around. 'You're sure Bigger let slip Vogler was aimin' to ride today?'

'Yeah. Maybe not in so many words, but that's what he implied.'

'I hope you're right. If this attack is gonna come, it'd be better if it came now when we're all up for it.'

Trueman grinned and laid a hand on Fiske's arm.

'Take it easy,' he said. 'You're worryin' too much. Vogler will be here presently, and we're prepared to meet him. There's nothin' else to do now but wait.'

'And maybe pray,' Fiske said. 'How's your wound, by the way?'

'It's sore, but it's nothin' much,' Trueman replied.

Fiske rode away to take up his own station and Trueman did likewise. He was positioned at the crest of the shelving bank of the stream. It wasn't high but it gave him a good prospect across the stream to the rolling rangeland beyond. He had brought his field glasses along with him and every so often he put them to his eyes to see if he could catch a first glimpse of Vogler's gunslingers, although Croft had been assigned the role of lookout. Perched in a tree further along, he had the best view and would raise the alarm. Trueman stretched full length on his good side. Strangholt's bullet had creased his shoulder, but fortunately it didn't affect his gun hand. If it had, the outcome of the subsequent shoot-out might not have been so favourable. He got out his pack of Bull Durham and twisted himself a cigarette. As he lit up and took his first drag, he found himself unaccountably thinking of Doc Drummond and Rose. How were they getting along on the wagon train? And were they missing their old house outside Dry Bluff? In the very short time he had spent there he had become quite attached to the place. Trueman suspected that their decision to move had not been taken lightly. It had probably been a long time gestating, and it had taken the events connected with Drummond's shooting to bring matters to a head. He had a sudden uprush of something he couldn't name: nostalgia, a sense of loss, a yearning for something? Whatever it was, it quickly passed. Among the bushes, birds were singing. A gentle wind brushed the branches of the trees. For the moment he was lulled into a sense of peace which a faint rhythmic drumming sound only served to intensify, till he heard Croft's voice calling:

'I see 'em. They're on their way.'

Instantly he was on his feet. He flicked the cigarette stub away, seized his rifle, and took up his position. He realized that the drumming sound that had entered his reverie was in fact the sound of hoofbeats, and as he listened it soon began to gather in volume. Although he could not see the others, he sensed a change in the atmosphere. The air was charged with a new sense of tension and he had a feeling that he was probably the only one not affected by it. Instead he felt a cool, clear-headed calm that the imminent presence of danger always seemed to produce and which had been the saving of his skin more times than he could recollect. It had been with him throughout the War, but it had been there even before. The sound of pounding hoofs grew steadily louder, and when he raised himself up he caught his first glance of the approaching horsemen.

It was hard to see just how many of them there were because of the haze they were creating, but there were plenty of them: more than he had reckoned on. As they approached the stream they began to slow down, most of them coming almost to a halt before entering the water.

As they did so, a figure suddenly appeared on the hither side of the stream. Trueman started in surprise as he recognized Fiske. What was going on? What was he doing? This wasn't part of the plan they had discussed. Fiske was carrying his rifle loosely as he advanced to the edge of the stream, and he called in a loud voice:

'Vogler! Turn round and go back. We don't want any trouble.'

There were a few moments of silence as his words hung in the air. Trueman looked intently at the group of riders on the far side of the stream, searching for Vogler. Trueman had only seen him once, but that was enough. He was waiting for a response to Fiske, but not in the form in which it came. Without warning, the silence was suddenly rent by the boom of a rifle shot and Fiske stumbled and fell. Although he was too far off to help, Trueman got to his feet as more shots rang out from among the ranks of the gathered horsemen. He didn't wait for any more indications of Vogler's intentions, but yelled out for everybody to hear:

'Open fire!'

Instantly, a fusillade of gunfire broke out from the bushes and trees along the banks of the stream and a number of Vogler's men slid from their saddles. The shooting was rapid and a huge wall of noise assailed the senses like a physical blow. At first Vogler's men made a relatively easy target, but after the opening salvo they began to move away and spread out, some of them dropping from their horses to take cover on the opposite side of the stream.

As the first wave of shooting subsided, Trueman looked for Fiske but couldn't see him. He could only hope that Fiske hadn't been badly hurt and had made it back into the shelter of the bushes. He felt at once both annoyed with and admiring of the foreman. His attempt to defuse the situation had been ill-advised, but it had taken courage to attempt it. In terms of the struggle which was now taking place, it hadn't made very much difference.

He jammed more slugs into his rifle and began

to fire once again. It was harder now to find a target and the general level of shooting was more irregular. As he looked up and down the stream his keen eyes detected movement further downstream, where the vegetation was particularly dense. A section of Vogler's men were crossing over, some on horseback and some on foot. Trueman squeezed off a couple of shots but quickly realized the gunnies were more or less out of range. It wouldn't do Fiske's cause any good if they were outflanked. Quickly coming to a decision, he began to move in their direction in an attempt to intercept them.

As he scurried along, taking care to take advantage of whatever cover offered itself, shots began to ring out and slugs sang through the air. Vogler's men had obviously spotted him and in a few moments he saw some of them. Sheltering behind a willow tree, he returned fire and saw two men fall to the ground. One of them began to crawl away into the safety of the undergrowth but the other one lay still.

Trueman raised his head and, seeing a rider just entering the water, squeezed off another shot. The man toppled sideways as the horse swerved. Another rider appeared and, quickly taking sight, Trueman was about to squeeze the trigger when he halted. The man was shouting something, then he turned and began ride away, following the line of the stream back in the direction Trueman had come from.

It was hard for Trueman to see just what was happening down by the water because bullets were continuing to wail around him, chopping down vegetation, and he sank to his knees to make himself less of a target. Another bullet thudded into a tree close by and sent shards of bark flying around him. Somewhere not far ahead someone had him in his sights. He lowered himself on to his face and began to crawl away, all the time trying to get a view of the man. Fortunately, there was a good deal of cover between him and his assailant.

When he was some yards clear of his original position he worked himself into a slight hollow from which he could watch. Shots were still ringing out but he couldn't see any further movement. What had happened to the man?

He was thinking about making another move when he detected a sudden quiver of the bushes and he had a brief glimpse of something blue: a man's shirt. He raised his rifle, waiting for it reappear, but instead he heard the bushes rustle and the sound of someone moving away through the trees. He waited a moment before quitting his temporary place of refuge, then raised himself up. The sounds of gunfire back along the stream-bank were fierce but when he moved to a place where he had a view across the stream, he was surprised to see that there was no longer any activity in his vicinity. He glanced back but could descry nothing in that direction.

He had anticipated that more of the gunnies would try to outflank Fiske's men and get behind them, but it seemed like Vogler had abandoned the enterprise. His own contribution to the conflict might certainly have held Vogler's men up, but he wasn't green enough to think he was responsible for the change. He waited and listened as the rattle of gunfire along the stream went on, and then, satisfied that there were no gunslicks left in his area, began to make his way back again.

When he had regained his former position he was able to take stock of the situation. Vogler's men seemed to be in a state of confusion. Men and horses lay thick on the ground, some wounded, some dead. Those gunnies who remained in the saddle were firing wildly in different directions, milling around and blasting away to little effect. Not wasting any time, he pumped a bullet into the rifle barrel and, lining his sights on one of the gunslicks, squeezed the trigger. When the smoke cleared he saw the man still sitting in the saddle, apparently unscathed, but while he was preparing to fire again the man raised his hand and, turning his horse, began to ride away.

In a few moments he was joined by a few others, while from the places where they had been hiding another half-dozen or so began to run, some seeking their horses, which had bolted in the furore. He watched as the gunslicks made their escape, hardly believing what he was seeing. Surely they hadn't given up the fight? Yet so it appeared. Shots pursued the disappearing gunnies and some of Fiske's men appeared by the stream, cheering and shouting. Among them were some people he didn't recognize. Who were they? He began to make his way down the sloping banks to join them, with one question drumming in his brain. What had become of Fiske?

Vogler had watched the progress of the battle by the stream with growing concern. At the first hint of trouble he had made good his escape, content to watch the affair from a safe distance. He had been taken by surprise, not expecting to meet any resistance. When it happened, after getting over his initial shock he still hadn't been too concerned. What sort of resistance could Fiske and his bunch of cow-hands put up against his gang of experienced gunslingers?

The longer the battle raged, however, the more worried he became. From his vantage point he had seen the unexpected arrival of a bunch of riders coming from the direction of Buzzard Roost. For a few consoling moments he had though it might be Bigger, Strangholt and Krall, maybe with a few others of their type they had picked up somewhere, but he soon realized he was mistaken. He didn't know who the newcomers were, but it quickly became apparent whose side they were on. Even before the remnants of his men began to waver and then break, he had turned his horse in the direction of the Buckle M.

It wasn't until he was a quarter-way back that he hit on a better plan. There was no knowing how some of his men might react. The Buckle M might not be the safest place to be, and besides, Fiske and his cowboys might decide to pay the Buckle M a visit. For the time being, at least, it might be advisable to make himself scarce. He thought briefly of the town of Buzzard Roost. There were places there he could hide out.

A little more thought persuaded him that a better place might be up in the hills where his stolen cattle were secreted, where some of his men were based, and where there was a remote cabin he could use. Yes, that was a better idea altogether. No one knew about the set-up there. He would be safe till things blew over and he could reorganize. Drawing his horse to a halt, he sat for a few moments weighing up the pros and cons before turning its head in the direction of the Bear Wallow foothills.

Trueman approached a group of men gathered by the stream, among whom he saw Morrison and Croft. He couldn't see Fiske, however, and he feared the worst. The men, however, were in jubilant spirits, which seemed to give the lie to his forebodings.

'Trueman!' Morrison greeted him. 'We were

wonderin' how you were.'

'What the hell is goin' on?' Trueman replied.

'The townsfolk swung it our way. I knew they would.'

'What do you mean?' Trueman asked.

'I told you some of them were about ready to take on Vogler. Well, I guess they proved it. They got here in the nick of time.'

Trueman looked about him. Among the Two Bar Cross ranch hands there were other men he didn't recognize. Most of them were still cheering and shouting. Then the truth finally dawned on him. They were from Buzzard Roost. Morrison had done his bit to arouse the townsmen and he had succeeded. It seemed their timely arrival had swung the outcome of the battle in their favour.

For a moment he felt something of the pride and relief they all felt, but it was short-lived as he thought of Fiske. He looked at Morrison.

'What about Fiske?' he said. 'What happened to him?' He was surprised to see a smile spread across the barman's features.

'Take a look,' Morrison said, pointing. 'He's right there.'

Trueman spun round. Sure enough, Fiske was there, sitting on a fallen tree branch, clutching at his shoulder, but alive. A couple of the townsmen stood beside him. One of them was carrying a knife, the other a flask. Trueman quickly made his way over and was greeted by the foreman with a wan smile and a nod of the head.

'It's good to see you, Trueman,' he breathed.

'Are you OK?' Trueman replied.

'I took a bullet. I've lost a lot of blood but I'll pull through. This gentleman is just about to cut it out.' Very gingerly Fiske lifted his shirt and Trueman caught a glimpse of the wound. The bullet had smashed Fiske's shoulder.

'It'll mend,' the man with the knife said. He turned to Fiske.

'I'm sorry, but this is gonna hurt.' The other man handed him the flask and he poured whiskey over his knife. 'Take a swig or two. I'll be as quick as I can,' he added.

Trueman turned away and walked down to the stream. The victors were continuing to celebrate but he wasn't as confident as they seemed to be. Sure, they had won but, until Vogler was accounted for and put behind bars, there was a chance his men might rally.

What had become of Vogler? He had seen no sign of him during the course of the fight. Had he even been there? Or was he back at the Buckle M? If that was the case, it might not be the best place to be if the surviving gunslicks turned up. He had a sudden insight. He and Fiske had seen Vogler the night they rode up into the hills. They had seen the cabin too. Wouldn't that be the logical place Vogler would head for? He would imagine himself safe enough up there. As far as he was concerned, no one knew about the cabin.

Trueman looked away towards the hills. It wouldn't take too long to ride out and take a look. If he was wrong, nothing was lost. In a matter of seconds he had taken the decision to check the cabin. He had only been there once, and in the dark, but he felt confident he could find it again. He glanced at the others, considering whether to inform them of his decision. They were still celebrating. He felt disinclined to go into the details of it all with anybody. Besides, he liked to ride alone. It would be simpler to just slip away. He moved swiftly along the stream bank and up through the bushes and trees till he reached the spot where his horse was tethered, climbed into leather and rode away.

At first he let the horse have its head. The wind blew in his hair and after his recent exertions, the ride was quite exhilarating. Following the riverbank, he reached a spot which he seemed to recognize as the place he and Fiske had crossed over the night they had visited the Buckle M. He steadied the Steel Dust through the shallows and up the slope beyond.

The hills grew steadily nearer, but even though Vogler's gunslicks had been defeated, he knew he might still be in danger because he was on Buckle M range. He kept a sharp lookout for any of Vogler's gunnies who might still be around but saw no one. Presently the trail started to climb as he reached the foothills and the Steel Dust began to flag. He brought it to a halt and slid from the saddle. While it rested and recovered its breath, he sat on the grass and built a smoke.

It was only then that the question struck him: what did he intend doing with Vogler once he found him? Well, since the citizens of Buzzard Roost had shown their true colours and stood up against Vogler, he could probably rely on the law to take its course. It struck him as odd that he was going up against someone he had not even met, but he only had to remember what had happened to Doc Drummond and the attempts that had been made on his own life to know why he was doing it.

When he had finished the cigarette he climbed back into the saddle and continued riding, taking care to let the horse pick its way at its own pace. He had little fear of losing his way. Like Fiske, once he had ridden a trail he didn't forget it. It was getting late in the day when he reached the rim of the valley and looked down on the cabin. This time, smoke was curling from the chimney and the light of a lamp glowed through the windows. Outside, in a small corral, a horse was grazing.

'Well,' Trueman said, addressing the Steel Dust, 'looks to me like someone is at home.'

He looked all round but could see no sign of anybody. The cattle had gone. Trueman guessed they had been moved to another hidden location.

He rode round the rim, examining the valley from different angles, but still couldn't see anybody. Choosing a spot which would bring him out at the rear of the cabin and hoping that way to avoid being seen, he began the descent to the valley.

He reached the valley floor, dismounted, and knee-haltered the Steel Dust. He looked up at the surrounding hills. Up there, it had been cool and breezy. Down here it was calm and still, but it would get cold when evening came on. The smoke was spiralling in the air from the cabin chimney. Vogler was making himself comfortable.

Trueman took a few moments to check his guns, then began to make his way towards the cabin. So far he had met with no opposition, but he remained alert and watchful. He reached the rear of the cabin and pressed close to the wall, listening. He could hear nothing. Swiftly and silently, he moved to the front and peered in at the window. There was a man sitting at a desk. He wore a frock-coat and when he turned his head towards him, Trueman knew it was Vogler. He ducked down, and then, drawing his six-gun, he kicked at the door.

It flew open. He was about to rush inside when some instinct warned him to hold back. Instead he moved sideways as a gun exploded from inside the house and bullets ripped through the air where a moment before he had been standing. He heard a rush of footsteps and a man appeared in the door-frame. It was only for a moment but it was long enough for Trueman to squeeze the trigger of his .44. There was a scream and a shout from inside the cabin and then the sound of something solid hitting the floor. Trueman rushed inside, fanning the hammer of his gun. A second man went down in a hail of lead, then there was silence. Trueman glanced at the table in the corner where he had seen Vogler sitting. The chair was vacant and Vogler himself had taken shelter under the table. As Trueman approached he began to whine and sob:

'Please. Don't shoot. Don't kill me.'

Trueman paused long enough to examine the two men lying on the floor, but he had nothing more to fear from them. Then he approached the whimpering figure of Vogler.

'Get up!' he snapped.

'Please! I'll give you anything you want. There's money in the safe. Take it. Just don't shoot.'

Trueman holstered his gun, then bent down and hauled Vogler to his feet. Vogler was shaking with fear.

'Who are you?' he managed to say.

'You don't need to know that.'

Sweat was running down Vogler's face. His mouth was quivering and he had developed a twitch in his cheek. Suddenly he began to weep.

'I know who you are. I know your name. You're Trueman.'

'And I know who you are,' Trueman replied.

'Please, I can make it worthwhile—'

'Shut up,' Trueman said. He gestured to Vogler to move, but Vogler was transfixed with fear. Trueman grabbed his arm and began to propel him towards the door.

'What are you going to do?' Vogler said. He began to plead again. 'Please, please don't kill me.'

'I ain't goin' to kill you,' Trueman said.

'What are you going to do? What—'

'I'm gonna take you in and hand you over to the law. Let the judge decide.' By dint of some pushing and pulling, he got Vogler out of the house and down to the corral.

'Get on your horse,' he ordered.

Once Vogler was in the saddle Trueman mounted up and they rode out, Vogler in front and Trueman just behind. The sun was getting low as they climbed the hillside and joined the trail leading around the rim of the valley. Vogler had gone quiet but from time to time his back shook as he let out a sob. When they reached the point at which he and Fiske had headed in the direction of the Falls, Trueman considered doing the same, but then opted to go down the way he had come up. He didn't know the state of play in town and it might be preferable to take Vogler back to the Two Bar Cross. When he was halfway down he realized he had made a mistake: he saw the riders.

There were five of them coming up the hill towards him and there was little doubt in his mind that they were Vogler's men. He expected Vogler to say or do something, but the man seemed too far gone in misery and despair to react. Truman spurred the Steel Dust forward and, seizing Vogler's reins, rode to where an outcrop of rock offered some cover. He slid from the saddle and pulled Vogler from his horse.

'Get down behind those rocks!' he snapped.

With a blow to their rumps, he sent the horses on their way. Taking cover himself, he drew his six-guns and watched for the riders' approach. The drumming of hoofs got louder and then the first of them appeared on the trail below him. He had been hoping they might ride on past, but instead reins jerked and hoofs dragged as the gunnies drew to a halt. Without preamble, their guns were in their hands and spitting lead. Bullets went singing all around, splintering the rocks behind which Trueman and Vogler crouched.

'Call them off!' Trueman shouted, but Vogler was in no state to respond. He thought for a moment of dragging Vogler to his feet and parading him in front of them, but it was too risky. The gunnies were firing wildly and they would both be shot.

Trying not to expose himself unduly, he peered round the rock, drew a bead on the nearest mounted gunslick, and pressed the trigger. He drew back instantly but when he had a chance to take another look, the horse was riderless. He caught a glimpse of another gunnie and triggered a quick one. The man clutched at his chest as his horse circled. Trueman sighted on him and fired again, then had to duck quickly as lead ricocheted around him. The gunslicks had the advantage over him and he really needed to get higher so he would be able to shoot down on them.

He looked about, looking for a way up that wouldn't leave him exposed, but no way presented itself. Another salvo of fire sent shards of rock flying around and he knew it could only be a matter of time before one of the enemy's bullets found its target. He started firing again, determined to at least make a show of it, but he knew they had him pinned down. His gun was empty and as he reloaded a bullet flattened itself an inch from his head. While most of the gunslicks' fire was wild and loose, one of them was getting too close. He guessed that the man had dismounted in an effort to get nearer.

Lying flat, he peered out, trying to pinpoint the gunman. Presently he thought he saw movement among a clump of boulders to his right. The man was in there, trying to creep up on him unawares. Taking careful aim, Trueman squeezed the trigger of his six-gun. There was a solid thud and a noise which was somewhere between a scream and a groan, and he knew he had found his target. He was expecting a response from the remaining gunslicks but it didn't come. Instead, their gunfire dwindled.

He counted quickly. As far as he could tell, he had probably accounted for three of them. That only left two. In the heat of the battle, he had neglected to take numbers into account. He was awaiting a fresh salvo of fire when he heard the whinny of a horse and then the sound of hoofs, which steadily receded before dying away.

He held his ground, not yet quite believing his luck, anticipating another round of gunfire. It didn't come and he realized that the two remaining gunnies had ridden away. The only explanation was that they had had enough. It seemed to encapsulate the day's events. They must have recognized Vogler, but they had still turned and fled. Vogler's reign was finally over. In the heat of the fight he had forgotten about Vogler. Now he turned to him in order to get on with the journey back to the Two Bar Cross once he had rounded up the horses.

'OK,' he said. 'Let's get goin'.'

There was no response. He assumed Vogler was still in a funk and bent over to shake him.

'I said let's go.'

Suddenly he pulled back his hand. It was wet. Trueman took a closer look. Vogler wasn't moving. He touched him again and Vogler's head flopped over, his blank eyes staring into emptiness. Blood flowed from a huge hole in his chest. He wouldn't face the verdict of the law after all. He had been shot by his own gunslicks.

When he was fully satisfied that the danger was over, Trueman emerged from cover and found the bodies of the three men he had shot. Two were lying where they had fallen from their horses and the third was lying among the rocks. They were all dead. He guessed they had not been among the group that had fought the battle at the ford. Maybe they had been left in charge of the stolen cattle. He looked about for the horses; it didn't take him long to locate them. Once he had done so he laid Vogler's body across his horse and then mounted his own to continue the ride back.

It was early in the morning and only one lamp was left to shed its light on the veranda of the Two Bar Cross where Trueman, Fiske, Croft and Morrison still remained. Sounds of celebration occasionally broke on their ears from the direction of the bunkhouse, but they were intermittent now.

'The boys sure made a night of it,' Croft said.

'They had a right to,' Fiske replied. He felt slightly awkward. Although they had come through the day's events with surprisingly few losses, not all of the ranch hands had survived. With some effort, he turned to Morrison.

'Guess they'll be celebratin' in Buzzard Roost,' he said.

'I reckon so. Vogler was like a yoke round their necks. Now they've thrown it off.' The barman rose to his feet. 'I guess I'd better be gettin' back to town myself.'

'Don't go now,' Fiske replied. 'You might as well bed down in the bunkhouse for the night. There's plenty of space.'

Morrison hesitated for a moment before sitting down again. He looked across at the foreman, whose shoulder was swathed in bandages. Trueman noticed that the barman seemed somewhat uncomfortable and, seeing his glass was almost empty, leaned forward and poured him another drink from the whiskey bottle standing on the table. Morrison took a swallow and seemed to gather himself.

'Matter of fact,' he said, 'that kinda brings me to somethin' I've been meanin' to mention.'

'What does?' Fiske said.

'You sayin' about the bunkhouse bein' empty. From what I've heard, I gather you've been findin' it hard to find men for the round-up and the cattle drive.'

'You could say that,' Fiske replied.

'Well, fact of the matter is, I was wonderin' if there might be a job here for me. I've about had it with bein' a bartender. I've got some experience. I worked on ranches long before becomin' a barman.'

Fiske leaned towards him, grimacing as a stab of pain shot through his shoulder.

'Of course,' he said. 'If that's what you want, I'd be right glad to take you on. Hell, I reckon you've earned it. Mind you, don't go gettin' the wrong idea. It's tough goin'.'

'Thanks. I sure appreciate it.'

Fiske nodded and turned to Trueman. 'What about you?' he said. 'I don't know what plans you have, but there's a job here for you too if you want it. I'd be glad to have you along.'

Trueman took a deep draught of whiskey before replying.

'That's real considerate of you,' he said, 'and I reckon I could do an awful lot worse. But just lately I've been thinkin' and I've got somethin' else in mind.'

'Yeah? What's that?'

'I told you all about what happened back in Dry Bluff, about how I came to be involved in all this in the first place. Well, those good friends I was tellin' you about are somewhere on a wagon train right now, headed for the Rocky Mountains, and I got a kind of yen to join 'em and go there myself.'

Fiske exchanged glances with the others.

'Haven't you had enough of travellin'?' he said. 'You've seen for yourself, it's real nice country round here. And we got mountains too. We got the Bear Wallows.'

'I wouldn't disagree with you there,' Trueman replied, 'but it ain't that. I don't know what it is. But once things here are finally settled, I aim to ride out and find that wagon train.'

Fiske grinned. 'Well,' he said, 'one thing's for sure. You won't have to worry about Vogler and his gunnies any more. Nor will anybody else.'

'You sure took a big risk tryin' to negotiate with 'em,' Trueman replied. 'You took us all by surprise when you stepped out right in front of those varmints.'

Fiske looked a little sheepish. 'I can see that now,' he said. 'I just figured I might still be able to make Vogler see sense. I guess I was only puttin' everyone at more risk.'

'Well, like you say, it's over now. Neither the Two Bar nor the town need worry any more about Vogler.' Trueman thought for a moment. 'And I guess that includes the good folk of Dry Bluff too.'

'Not to mention those wagon trains,' Croft added.

'I've heard the days of the wagon train are just about over,' Trueman replied, 'so I guess it won't make much difference there. I guess I ain't gonna get many other chances to travel that way.'

Following his words they lapsed into silence. The sounds from the bunkhouse had finally ceased. The moon and stars poured down their light and nature's calm did what it could to salve the wounded world. Eventually Croft sat up and poured himself another drink.

'You'll see,' he remarked. 'Whether it's the wagon train or somethin' else, there'll always be varmints like Vogler and his gang lookin' to cause trouble.'